THE

GRASSHOPPERS

COME

THE
GRASSHOPPERS
COME

DAVID GARNETT

BREWER, WARREN & PUTNAM

WOOD ENGRAVINGS BY

R. A. GARNETT

THE
GRASSHOPPERS
COME

There was a withered yellow tip to every reed so that each one was partly dead even though it was still growing, and these yellow tips made an autumnal landscape in the heat of June. When a breath of wind came to bend them down, the reeds at one moment were all yellow, and then, as they stooped lower under the caress, grey-green.

They grew in the soft clay along the river for a hundred miles, in beds that were a mile across on each side, so that the river was lost in them and no man or beast in that empty land of the tundras could approach it.

Overhead the sun shone in a cloudless sky. You

might ride all day and the day after before you came to men or cattle; but in the river the sturgeon swam and in the reeds a few unmated storks still lingered sadly. All day long the bed of reeds was filled with a sound which was so monotonous and unceasing that like the heat of the sun and the blueness of the sky and the yellow tips of the reeds, it determined the character of the place itself.

This sound was the stridulation of grasshoppers, or locusts, gathered into a choir so vast that the chirrup of individuals was not noticeable: the sound was not altered perceptibly when the nearest of them fell silent. Sometimes one of the musicians would crawl higher than usual on a reed, right up to the yellow tip, and after clinging there and stridulating, would spread out his flat wing-cases, and with a whirr of gauzy underwings and a big jump, would fly off aimlessly and after a few yards flop so heavily among the reeds that it was a wonder that his brittle joints were not broken. Sometimes, however, they were, and the maimed creature would sink lower and lower down among the reeds and disappear.

Each day as the sun sank the grasshoppers would climb up the reeds until the yellow tips were thick with insects, and when it set, with millions of little horny eyes they gazed at the vanishing rim, and then, clinging tighter, they swayed with the reeds throughout the night, motionless until dawn broke and drew their eyes to the east, to catch sight of the first flames.

In the twilight and before the dawn the rare storks moved like pale ghosts among the reeds, busily employed with their long sword-shaped bills among the frozen sun-worshippers.

But each day as the sun grew hotter with the advance of summer, more and more grasshoppers would open their wings and launch themselves into the air and, with many blind collisions, would rise higher in little whirling eddies that drifted with the wind over the tops of the reeds before they sank down again. Often, when a little bunch of four or five fell clumsily together in one spot, it would startle an insect that had been stridulating there into a short outlying flight, so that, when one of these incipient swarms subsided and pattered down among the reeds, it threw up a few more flying insects like splashes of mud on a dirty road.

As each day of the early summer passed, the sun grew hotter, the fine windless weather more settled, and the stridulation noisier, more incessant, and the little whirlpools, which seemed to catch up the flying insects over the reeds, larger and more powerful, holding them up longer in flight.

The green of the great field was vivid. About it, on two sides, were fringes of low oak trees the leaves of which still had a tawny tinge in them as though they had been chapped with chilblains by the late frosts of May. Facing the oak trees were rows of corrugated iron sheds with asphalt in front of each running down into the vivid grass, and the long arms and pipes of giant scarlet or yellow petrol pumps stood beside their huge doorways like etiolated sentries mounting guard.

The fourth side of the great field was bounded by a low wire fence, with a row of newly built, red-tiled little houses on the far side of a black main road. Not far off the electric trams started, for the huge field was on the outskirts of a big town.

From a mast over the Tudor Cottage Club-house, and from four other lower ones set in the middle of each of the four sides of the field there streamed tubular banners which were blown out by the summer wind.

The air was full of sound. Through all the hours while daylight lasted, now near, now deafening, now a mere weary buzzing more remote, there roared the aero engines and the shuddering tune of whirling propellor tips. The sky vibrated ceaselessly with noise that beat down and shattered the peace of the summer day.

Men in blue or khaki overalls came and went, moved lazily about the sheds, came out on to the asphalt and looked up briefly at the sky, while, with scarcely a pause, the great engines tore in circles round the aerodrome, lifted a few hundred feet into the air by the light wood and linen wings they dragged with them.

There were half a dozen aeroplanes flying at once for most of the day, painted in different colours, blue and white, yellow and white, or grey all over, and marked with different letters. Some of them were biplanes, some monoplanes, and from their bodies could be seen sometimes one head and sometimes two protruding, either side by side or one behind the other.

Round and round they flew, some higher up wandering off a little way over the surrounding country, others lower down, and these lower machines were continually shutting off their engines and gliding almost silently in to land, dropping their tails as they settled down and bounced upon the earth, when, after a short run, they stopped until suddenly the engine was opened up again, and they would roar across the grass into the eye of the wind and fly away.

Every half-hour or so each of these machines would come spluttering noisily, bouncing across the grass, taxying to the sheds, and one of the men in it would unfasten his telephone and climb awkwardly out of the rear cockpit and walk slowly to the club-house. While he was still grinning and unbuckling his helmet, another pupil would be strapping himself into the vacant seat, and an overalled mechanic would lift up the tail and wheel the machine round for it to taxy out to the leeward side of the aerodrome.

Occasionally in the course of the day a strange machine which had come from some distant aerodrome would appear high up and slowly descend, gliding with many turns until it was low enough to make the last low left-hand turn and glide softly over the tops of the squat oak trees, and float lower and lower on to the grass which it would touch gently, running forward for a little, before it taxied to the sheds. A weary man would climb out and walk rather stiffly up to the mechanic, who approached him. 'Petrol.'

Wright, the ground engineer at the Swynford Club Aerodrome, and his mate Bill smiled gently over their morning's work. Bill was monkeying with the dynamo of Mr. Sefton's car which was not charging the battery properly, while Wright was tracing out the cause of an intermittent miss on the starboard magneto of a Gipsy engine and was toying with a pair of feeler gauges. Both of them were free for a little while from interference and they worked soberly and happily. Wright never hurried over his work, and if the Club Secretary or one of the instructors came in to watch him impatiently, he would knock off work at once or find himself another job. As he was a good man with a good record, they let him alone.

On a busy afternoon, of course, things were very different. Wright in his long yellow coat would spend his time running from machine to machine, to lift the tail of one, to hang desperately on to the end of a wing, while the machine was skidded round by a burst of engine, and then stand for a moment with his long black hair blown up on end, and the skirt of his yellow dust-coat fluttering in the slip-stream of the propellor, watching the 'plane lumbering off across the grass before he turned to meet another machine, taxying in after a pupil's solo flight.

There was always an indelible pencil behind Wright's ear; he had to sign chits, detach counter-foils, enter times of departure and hand over receipts at every moment. The fine summer months, with their lengthened hours of daylight, were spent in unceasing work, and he looked forward to the dark, fog-bound December days as the happiest time of the year, and the prolonged equinoctial gales when there was no flying at all were welcome. When the rain lashed wildly on the window-panes and drummed on the galvanised hangar roofs, he could find opportunities to undertake a big overhaul, but in June there was flying every afternoon and all day on Sunday, so that there was only an hour or two each day when he could stoop over the bench and forget the outside world, whistling plaintively to himself and thinking, not so much with his brain, as with his fingers, aided by a score of gauges, dies, calipers and machine tools.

Having traced out the short in the dynamo, Bill drifted slowly by Wright's bench eyeing the dismantled engine.

'Seen the paper, chum?'

A shake of the head answered him.

'A Sidestrand crashed up in Scotland, near Rosyth.'

'That'll be a hell of a mess. The Air Force is having a bad time this spring.'

'Well, what d'you expect?' asked Bill, moving on. 'I'll just have time to change that tail-skid Mr. Sykes was complaining about, before lunch.' Wright nodded and sighed again. The paradise of his dreams, which was filled with aeroplanes in perfect condition that never had to leave the ground, was very far away. He was more afraid of crashes than any of the pilots who went up in the machines, and for ten minutes, after Bill had set to work on the skid, the burnt-out wreckage of the Sidestrand came between Wright and his work. But at last the plaintive whistling, like the pipe of a solitary bullfinch in its cage, began again—a sign that the ground engineer had lost consciousness of himself and had fallen into a trance over the ignition system, thinking with his hands.

The telephone bell rang.

'Wreaks speaking. Tell Mrs. Johnson that Mrs.

Beanlands and Commander Shap are coming down for lunch in the club-house. We have had a favourable weather report and I am to try and get her unstuck this afternoon, so have the old bus out, and fill her up full.'

Wright's hand shook as he put back the receiver. All his peace was gone, and his appetite for lunch as well. Mrs. Beanlands' long-distance special monoplane carried a full load of 1900 gallons of petrol and had already been nearly wrecked once by running into the far hedge of an aerodrome. The big crash Wright was dreading was timed for that afternoon.

Jimmy Wreaks, the tall one-eyed man with the scars on his face and hands and the broken nose, sat on the edge of the little basket-work chair smiling nervously out of politeness. His smile was a mistake. It showed a hole where a tooth was missing in the lower jaw and a long yellow eye-tooth dropping down from the upper one to fill the gap, and, after revealing what would better have been kept hidden, this unfortunate smile came violently in contact with the tight knot of a scar in the middle of his cheek and was cut off sharp.

They were sitting over luncheon in the club-house. On Jimmy's right was his employer, Mrs. Beanlands, and facing him Commander Shap who was speaking.

'. . . a toast we must all drink: may we beat the long-distance record!' He rose, lifting his glass of champagne, and Jimmy rose and Mrs. Beanlands rose, flushed and rather pretty.

All three stood in silence, clinked glasses and drank and in silence sat down. The champagne bottle was finished. These three were starting that afternoon in *The Wayzgoose*, a big monoplane built to break the world's record for a long-distance flight. It was their fourth attempt to start. On the first occasion they had run into the far hedge of a smaller aerodrome narrowly escaping total destruction, and on the second and third Wreaks had turned back, once because of fog, once for very little cause that he could explain. But as there was a violent storm in Germany that day they forgave him, though they could hardly give him credit for foretelling it two hours before, on the east coast of England.

After so many false starts it was difficult for them to feel sure that they were really off. Shap might be filling up glasses and saying: 'Here's to better luck next time,' at nine o'clock that night. They did not even feel sure that the newspaper men would turn up to photograph the start of the flight. They were aware that they were becoming figures in an old story. Moreover, who cared about long-distance flights any longer? There had been too many of them.

'Now you must have a Benedictine each and a cigar, or your pipes just as you prefer,' said Mrs. Beanlands. 'It will be your last smoke for ever such a long time. Let that make it especially precious to you. So just take whichever you like best.'

'Er. Thank you. I will, please,' said Wreaks, holding out his white-scarred hand to take a half a Corona from the box, reflecting that he was not going to be intimidated because a rich woman made an awful fuss over standing him an extra one and sixpence. However dirty the other parts of Jimmy got with ingrained oil, the terrible white patches on the backs of his hands and wrists remained spotless. They marked the places where his flesh had been burnt away when he had fought his way out of a blazing aeroplane, and then into it again, to rescue his observer, in 1917.

Mrs. Beanlands knew his history: of proven heroism greater than that in any legend, of matchless skill, of deathless courage, of incredible escapes. . . . She admired the man and she pitied him, but for some time past she had regretted having engaged him.

When Wilmot Shap had first found Wreaks they had both felt that they were marvellously lucky to have secured him. But the flight had been put off so long, ever since March, and she had got to feel the scars and the smile, the yellow tooth and the patch over the eye, very trying indeed.

It was so tiresome for Wilmot and her to have a man of another class with them. Unfortunately they needed a pilot as well as a navigator. It would have been perfect if she and Wilmot could have gone off alone: she had several times been near suggesting it, but she knew that it would not be reasonable or fair to dear Wilmot to make such a proposal. As it was she could not very well engage another pilot instead of Wreaks. He was well known, and she had signed a tiresome contract with him.

Mrs. Beanlands was a fluffy-haired woman of forty, who had come into great wealth on her husband's death. For ten years she had been a faithful, loving and devoted wife, and suddenly, when she had given up all hope of leading an adventurous life of her own, she had come into her reward. Alfred had died, and six months afterwards she had met Wilmot on the Riviera, at Monte Carlo in fact, and the happiest intimacy, the most marvellous romantic adventure, had come out of that meeting.

Lily Beanlands drained the last drop of her glass of Benedictine, looked at her flushed face in a tiny mirror and, rising up from the table, left the two gentlemen to themselves. They hated each other and had nothing to say, so they just lapped up the last of the Benedictine and smoked their cigars.

Wilmot Shap was very dark with such liquid black eyes, so blue a jaw, such well-brushed black hair, that he looked like a sleek water animal, with a wet black coat, ready to plunge into the stream and vanish quickly without leaving a ripple on the surface. There was something adaptable, sinuous and soft about his personality; it was impossible to think of his glossy fur being rubbed up the wrong way. He was a gambler, he had lived all his life by gambling; he was gambling at that moment.

⁂

'See you back sometime in August, I suppose,' said Wright the ground engineer. Wreaks smiled.

'You won't leave us all that time hanging out to dry on the far hedge, will you?' he replied, and without waiting to listen to the answer, he climbed rapidly into the front cockpit and gently pushed the throttle open to its full extent.

The 560 h.p. engine roared so that the earth

shook and the hangars seemed to waver like packs of cards in the hands of a skilful shuffler; the blast of the slip-stream tore up grass and dirt and covered the photographers with fragments. An onlooker's hat flew away and crumpled itself up round a petrol pump. All thoughts and images in the minds of the three were cut off short: the very faculty of thinking was suspended by the sound which transformed human consciousness to a tight ball of endurance and all outside it to a jelly. The gross physical vibration of sound shook its way through the protective fibres of leather helmet, beat on the ear-drum, and the living brain trembled and shook against the sounding-box of the skull.

Wreaks closed the throttle. Mrs. Beanlands' head drooped forward with relief and then she remembered to look about her and smile brightly. Wreaks waved a gloved hand; mechanics pulled away the chocks and suddenly the engine roared again, the 'plane moved forward, the tail went up and the machine rushed forward with them into the wind's eye.

'It seems queer to be setting out on such a voyage,

on such a summer afternoon,' Mrs. Beanlands was thinking at that moment. 'It would be more natural at night, or very early in the morning.'

For forty seconds Commander Shap sat without breathing, gripping the side of the fuselage, with lips parted, teeth clenched, eyes staring. He was afraid.

His sense impressions were broken into discontinuous drops or globules in the agony of anticipating a horrible death. Sight, hearing, smell, taste and touch, all had become intermittent.

Mrs. Beanlands turned to him as the machine raced over the sward and tapped him on the elbow, but he did not feel her touch and his staring eyes never moved. She smiled to herself.

'Dear Wilmot! How deeply he feels the romance of this adventure. It's such a thrilling moment, if only we don't have to turn back again.' She was thinking this in the moments of their greatest danger.

The 'plane was running very fast, and Wreaks could feel that a large part of the immense weight was air-borne. He sat perfectly still, holding the stick just a little forward, determined that at all costs he would not let the machine bump hard after she had once lifted. They had not carried such a full load on any of the previous trials. Suddenly Wreaks knew that the machine was going to fly off and he smiled slightly. Two hundred yards from the hedge he relaxed his slight forward pressure on the stick and at once the machine lifted.

Bump! They touched once and they were off. They cleared the hedge by a yard or two and travelled, roaring as they went, through the air, low down over a big arable field. To the nearest spectators it seemed as though they were going to crash, when they were really gathering speed. Wreaks was looking at the A.S.I. (air-speed indicator) and watching the hand creep down to the right: 90-92-95-100. He caressed the forward edge of the stick, *stroking* it back, and the machine at once gained a little height while the hand of the A.S.I. travelled back rather fast: 100-95-90-85. Without hurrying, he pressed the stick a trifle forward. They would clear the trees which stood between them and the estuary and once they had crossed the belt of low oaks, the ground sloped away from under them and they gained height relatively.

Shake a tube full of dusty little blobs of mercury and suddenly the film of dust which holds one apart from the other breaks down, and in place of a string of beads you have a silver column. Your necklace of beads has become all one thing, which expands and contracts as one and measures the outside world to a nicety.

Wilmot Shap was smiling; he turned to Lily Beanlands with a laugh. 'We hadn't much to spare, but we are all right now.'

Only one globule of mercury remained separate for longer than the others before it broke into the silvery river. Shap became aware of an ache in his left hand and let go of the fuselage with stiffened paralysed fingers. The tendons in his wrist were a little strained. All was over: all was well.

They were crossing the mudbanks of the estuary; they were over the water. Wreaks was coaxing the machine gently round in a slow left-hand turn.

Soon Shap would glance at the first of his file of maps and would mark a compass bearing.

The sky was blue, the sun shining brightly a little behind them on the right-hand side. When Shap looked over the edge he could see their shadow on the left and rather in front of them running along the gleaming mudbank. It was low tide; a tug was steaming downstream, her wake spread out over the surface like a half-closed fan. In front of them was the large red square of the Swynmouth Haven Hotel standing among trees on a cliff overlooking the sea.

Wreaks looked at the sea in front and the ships dotted about in it, then he glanced at the compass by his left knee and followed the line of the centre of the estuary. He was barely 400 feet over the water and decided not to try and gain any more height. If the engine failed they would drown at whatever height they were, but there was not the slightest reason why a Napier Lion fresh from being vetted by Wright should fail. He lifted his hand to the knob of the throttle and gently slid it back, watching the revolution counter as he did so. When the needle was flickering over the figure 21 (2100 revs. a minute) he was satisfied, and looked out once more at the horizon. Then he turned in his seat and caught Shap's eye.

Though the monoplane had been designed originally as a two-seater, the rear cockpit had been enlarged and room had been made in it for two slightly staggered seats. In the forward left-hand one sat Shap and looking over his right shoulder was Mrs. Beanlands who was able by putting her feet up, to lie very nearly at full length. All the pilot's instruments for flying were of course in the front cockpit. Besides the usual instruments the dash was thick with gadgets: for instance there were no less than four separate thermometers recording temperatures of mixture, oil, water and carburettor.

Wreaks regarded most of these devices with scorn: 'Two carburettor thermometers and no wireless. How's that, eh? And do you know why? Because darling Wilmot couldn't be bothered to learn to use a wireless receiver. But they've made up for that in the front cockpit; the chap who designed that instrument panel didn't know I had got only one eye.'

An elaborate system of speaking-tubes had been installed. One pair of tubes connected the front cockpit with the rear. When Commander Shap or Mrs. Beanlands plugged in their telephone connections they could listen to what Wreaks said and could reply through a common mouthpiece. Mrs. Beanlands had to lean forward a little to reach this.

Since they were both in the same cockpit they could have made each other hear by shouting, but it would have been very exhausting and would have prevented their conversing on a long flight. For this reason a second pair of tubes had been installed into which they could plug their telephones to talk to each other. Wreaks was not connected up with these tubes and when he wished to speak had to turn his head or wave his arm to attract their attention after which they would plug in to listen to him. This arrangement of the speaking-tubes greatly increased the privacy of the rear cockpit and added to the estrangement of pilot and navigator.

Directly Shap saw the head in the cockpit in front of him turn round, he plugged his telephone into the tube to speak to him and corked up the other tube so Lily should not have the roar of the engine in her ears.

'Well, you took off marvellously, Jimmy,' he said. 'We're well away now. Aren't you going to take her up to 1000 feet?'

'No. Not till we get a bit lighter. I am leaving land at Bosworth coastguard station and setting a course five points north of east.'

'Right-o, I'll mark it.'

Lily Beanlands pulled out a stopper in the speaking-tube, and for a moment there was a roar in the pilot's ears interrupting his conversation and then the unpleasant scrape of metal as she plugged in.

'What a glorious take off, Jimmy! We are actually crossing the beach now. Do you realise? So it's good-bye to old England. Good-bye. Good-bye!'

'Yes. We're off at last,' answered Wreaks. The

machine hit a bad bump as they left the cliff behind them and he corrected the lateral trim gently and firmly with a sideways pressure of the stick. Then he glanced at the compass again before he spoke.

'I expect to cross the Dutch coast at Alkmaar,' he said. 'We ought to do it in about an hour and twenty minutes.'

'Aren't you going higher up over the sea?' asked Lily.

'No. We may gain height gradually as we lose weight. At present we are too overloaded for it to be worth while to climb.' There was a silence.

'Oh, look! What a sweet boat! Like a toy,' said Lily. The men politely looked, bending their heads to look over the side directly down. Underneath them the men in the dinghy gazed up, their red upturned faces were bright spots against the greeny-blue sea. Beyond them a tug was setting out to sea, and the black mass of smoke pouring from the funnel preceded the little boat in a dirty ravelled fog over the blue waves, blown far ahead of her on her journey.

'Look at that for a west wind. Just what we want,

a tail wind to help us on our way. We shouldn't have got off the ground so easily if it hadn't been for this wind,' said Wreaks to himself, but he did not remark on it to the others.

England was behind the aeronauts and already forgotten by them. They did not turn their heads for a last view of it. Before them a faint scum of dirtiness seemed to have gathered over the rim of the sea.

The pupils at the flying club swooped one after another silently upon the porridge-coloured grass of the aerodrome, touched the wheels of the machines and bounced and bumped about on the ground for a moment before pushing the throttle wide and roaring off. . . .

Round and round the Moths circled, never still for long; never content to rest, until many hours later with folded wings they were packed close upon each other and left in the darkness of the hangars.

In Asia the locusts whirled round and round in the late afternoon, pattering down on the dry reeds and startling other locusts into spasmodic flight.

The great monoplane roared through the air towards the east.

When they reached Holland the land, even from a height of only 500 feet, was hazy and blurred with the milkiness of mist. Yet it was only half-past three and the sun was still quite high up. There were people on the sands, children paddling and looking up at them, and a motor car ran along a road. But the whitish mist combined with the sunshine made everything seem unreal.

'Well, the most dangerous part of the trip is over,' said Shap, plugging in so that he could hear Wreaks reply.

'That's right. It's always nicer to feel that one can get down if one must. I believe this is just south of Alkmaar. Look and see if there isn't a big canal that turns in towards the town on the map. I guess that's it.'

Holland was an unreal world seen through smoked glass; a fogged plate with everything blurred and indistinct. Wreaks brought the machine still lower, but the ground did not gain reality as they approached it.

Black and white cattle threw up their tails and galloped on stiff-jointed legs scattering to the corners of the field, terrified by the giant above them. A pony drawing a hooded gig jogged along a narrow interminable road, and a woman in a sun-bonnet peered up at them from under the edge of the hood. She was holding the reins in her left hand. Tumbrils loaded with hay crossed the fields; from a haystack a man waved his prong and the pale sun cast a gleam on the steel points.

Shap suddenly became very busy map-reading and reporting their exact position to Wreaks. Lily Beanlands lay back in her seat with a smile of beatitude on her face. She was thinking: 'I am free now. It's funny to think that I am flying away from all of them—flying to fame. How silly Eileen's tennis seems now! And yet the fact that she was going to play in the Bournemouth tournament used to come before everything. Our whole lives were planned in the hopes that Eileen should get into the mixed doubles at Wimbledon, and she never did and never will.

We all had to think of Eileen all the time and, of course, none of them ever guessed what was in me. Even I never really quite believed that I was going to do something really great like this.

Well, now they'll know.

I'm happy at last after all those awful years when I was supposed to be a kitten: Alfred's kitten and Eileen's doormat. The boys were just as bad as Eileen really with Rugby and rock-climbing and winter sports.

'Good-bye, Lily. Sorry you always have to be left behind. It's hard luck. Good-bye, Lily. Don't get into mischief. Don't get too bored without us if we get snowed up for a couple of days in that beastly hut. So long, Lily, be good.'

It was silly of me to mind so much; I am much too sensitive, and I think I am rather romantic and proud with a streak of something wild. . . .

Since she had nothing better to do, and Wilmot was busy with his map, she thought about her own wildness for some time and then fell into a doze. For most of the time she was still aware that she was in her own aeroplane flying across Europe to break the long-distance record, but for a few minutes her mind slipped off to an odd, unpleasant memory. She believed that she was awake, so she could not be dreaming, at the same time she could not control her thoughts.

She was in a country-house with her stepchildren. . . . It was just before Guy Fawkes Day. A motor klaxon screamed wildly, and as a car pulled up a boy and a girl of about twenty jumped out and charged up to the front door and pealed the bell. As the parlourmaid opened the door there was a noise of nailed boots clattering down the stairs at full speed, and as the elder children entered, a younger figure on the stairs charged down on them.

There were yells of delighted laughter: young Leslie was wearing a comic mask with beetroot-pink cheeks and black whiskers. A moment later their father appeared on the landing of the stairs. His mask was appalling—an upturned Slavonic nose spreading bulbously on one side, a beetling forehead overhanging a pair of squint Mongolian eyes, while below sagged a pair of false indiarubber lips.

Lily followed him from her bedroom with a demure tread to welcome the children back. She had just powdered her face after wiping off the skin-food. Her complexion could hold its own with any girl's. A yell of delight greeted her, a yell which was followed by a momentary, appalling silence. Then Alfred pulled off his mask and began asking heartily about the journey. She kissed Eileen. John kissed her. Then as she followed Alfred into the dining-room she caught a whisper from the girl to her brother as they were hanging up their coats. 'That last phiz was the best of the three. D'you know I didn't recognise her. . . .'

Just as they reached the outskirts of Hamburg they ran into rain.

'I'm going right up out of this mess,' said Wreaks. 'I don't like it at all.' He pressed his fingers gently back against the stick as though he were stroking a cat's throat and they rose, and as he did so he watched the needle of the A.S.I. travel back. It was travelling back fast, for they were very heavy and climbed with difficulty.

'We don't want to get all wet,' he thought, and pushed the knob of the throttle forward. 'I'll go up as fast as I can.'

The A.S.I. needle steadied itself and stopped at 90. The revolution counter showed 2250. The altimeter was trembling over the 1000-foot mark. Outside the cockpit nothing was visible; a white and clammy cloud enveloped them. 'This cursed weather must have been travelling down the Rhine,' he thought. 'The wind will have turned a bit southerly, we must allow for that.' He glanced casually at the turn indicator and inclinometer: the machine was level laterally.

Suddenly the cloud in which they were wrapped lightened. There was a whiteness ahead of them, sunshine behind them, a rainbow leapt against a cloud. They came out of the white fog into the blue sky, and as far as the eye could see, for hundreds of square miles stretched an immense snowfield, or ice-floe, of crystalline white cloud which seemed solid. Only rarely did it reveal a fluffy or woolly edge. This plain of snow was not continuous and smooth but like a Polar sea of ice, made up of tables and flattened ridges with fissures between them, but nowhere was there a hole through which one might catch a sight of the earth.

The scene was wildly pretty, like the heaven of the most heavenly Christmas pantomime, or a Victorian coloured stereoscopic view of Switzerland. But it was desert, desert as the moon. The pantomime chorus, dressed as angels with blue ribands and gold crowns: they weren't there. The sun blazed in a heaven of deep forget-me-not blue and threw the shadows of the heads of the travellers on to the cockpit dash in front of them. On the farthest horizon a range of majestic mountains rose up above the snowfield like Alpine peaks.

Lily Beanlands woke up. 'Oh, oh,' she whimpered. 'What a horrid brown study to fall into! What a horrible mask Alfred had put on, and poor Eileen. . . . It was almost like a dream . . . and it's odd because none of it ever happened, did it?'

She collected herself. Wilmot was bending towards her. She felt that to have fallen asleep would have been unpardonable. It would have shown no feeling for romance; it would have been a neglect of duty and a confession of age. Wilmot must not think that she had fallen asleep when she was only musing on the unhappy past.

She looked about her and suddenly realised that they were flying above the clouds. Shap was plugging in to talk to her.

'Isn't it exquisite up here?'

'How high are we?' she asked, feeling that it was a safe question.

'Four thousand. But though our speed drops a little as we climb, we are much better off out of the rain, and Wreaks told me he was going to fly at this altitude until just before sunset when I shall make an exact determination of longitude. If the weather is clear he intends to come down to confirm my observations by spotting some town or river or railway and then he'll take us up again for the night. And I can check our position at intervals by star observations.'

They relapsed into silence.

There was so much time before them that they both felt that they must be economical of their enthusiasms and their talk, lest they should exhaust all possibility of amusing and entertaining each other. So Lily Beanlands spent several hours happily looking at the golden sunlight and the white floor of the clouds and then at the great powerful wing and the instruments on the dash. Hours went by, smiles and words were exchanged, and slowly the sun sank behind them and the white mountains ahead of them became tinged with pink reflections.

They had forgotten the passage of time; they were lulled and hypnotised by the engine whose voice in their ears had sunk from the first deafening roaring to a faint bubbling drone, which at last was itself but scarcely heard. Yet though unheard, it dominated them, determining their mood. Everyone who has lived beside a waterfall will have had this experience. The roar of the torrent fades until only the tiny irregular noises in the flow are heard and these fade at last into a dream. But if the thoughts wander too far and impose a new mood on the dreamer the sound of the cataract returns suddenly in all its violence, jealous of new images which it drowns and washes from the mind.

Jimmy Wreaks turned in his seat. Shap was looking over the edge into vacancy, and the pilot could not attract his attention, so he closed the throttle and put the nose of the machine down. Directly afterwards he opened the throttle again and levelled out. By the time he had done this, Shap was asking him what was wrong.

'Couldn't get you to notice me,' shouted Wreaks

cheerfully. 'I want you to take a sextant reading, please.'

Shap felt unreasonably resentful at being woken from his day-dream and reminded of his duties by such drastic means, but he did not show he was annoyed.

'I'm afraid you will have to put the machine off her course, so I can get the sun without twisting right round in my seat.'

Wreaks banked sharply, and they swung round with a dipping wing. The sun was low down, and Shap busied himself for some time with his instruments. When he had made his readings, Jimmy banked the other way and swung back on to the original course.

'Between 54 and 55 latitude; and 18 longitude by the chronometer,' said Shap. 'I can't tell the latitude very exactly.'

'Where is it on the map?'

'About sixty miles north-west of Danzig, on the coast-line.'

'We can't be as far as that,' said Wreaks. 'Not

unless we've had a most tremendous tail-wind all the way. Anyway I am going down to see.'

The setting sun was striking upon a far range of snow mountains, turning them to gold and scarlet, and the snowfield beneath paled to an ashy grey. Mrs. Beanlands and Commander Shap twisted themselves round in their seats to look at the red ball of the setting sun, and the slip-stream caught their raised heads, buffeting the raised tops of their helmets, insinuating itself in icy wedges under the protecting collars of fur, and reminding them, what they had almost forgotten, that they were in the air.

The tail fin and elevators were brilliantly clear-cut and black against the red sunset. Mrs. Beanlands noticed a frail wire leading to the rudder and sighed. Life was so wonderful! Everything was so marvellous! Wilmot's hand was resting on her elbow. This was first love! This was a wonderful comradeship!

The Baltic air drove like a wedge of ice into her great fur collar and stung her neck with cold. She looked at the black bars of cloud, at the red ball of the sun, at the black elevators, and moved her arm to lay her hand gently on Wilmot's wrist.

Wreaks closed the throttle and startled her with the silence. The aeroplane was descending in a long glide, which seemed as though it might last for ever. The relief of silence was extraordinary. She looked at Wilmot and laughed, and he laughed back.

A few wisps of cloud caught the machine; it rocked violently, and down below, in front of them, appeared a level expanse of grey and empty sea and far away, ahead of them, a line of white breakers and a bar of sand or shingle projecting far out. The sun had set. It was eight o'clock.

'It's where I said it was,' shouted Shap. 'That's the Putziger Bank. We're over the gulf of Dantzig.'

'Good enough,' replied Wreaks. 'We've done wonderfully. I'm going up again now to get what's left of that tail-wind.'

The roar of the engine fell on them like the weight of a heavy pack taken up again at the end of a day's walk. For a while the sound cut cruelly into their nerves, then they forgot it and did not hear it. The bumps died away as they climbed again above the cloud.

The sky was full of stars; the earth below invisible except at long intervals when rare lights shone out also in that lower darkness. But the sky was transparent, even in its obscurity. It was very blue.

Wilmot Shap and Mrs. Beanlands began talking.

'What about some food?' she suggested. 'Will you have a sandwich or some of the hot coffee?'

It was delightful to move about a little in her seat groping for the parcel and the thermos. She snuggled down as low as she could, thinking: 'How cosy one can be. A woman like me can make any place that she is in seem like home.'

The hot coffee spilled on their lips and was blown out of the corners of their mouths.

Shap shouted jovially to the pilot: 'We're having supper. When are you going to have some?'

'No thanks. I'm all right. I'm going to have some coffee presently.'

While in the rear cockpit Wilmot and Lily crouched and gossiped and ate their sandwiches, throwing tight balls of crunched-up paper out into the darkness and whirlwind of the sky, Wreaks sat motionless scanning the illuminated dash in front of him with his one eye. Everything was going very well. Engine and oil and all the host of temperatures were quite healthy. 'I feel like a bloody research engineer in this outfit,' he said to himself. 'But God knows what it's all for. I can't put anything right if they go wrong. A chap might do a hurried forced landing and then discover it was only a broken thermometer that was wrong.'

After the sandwiches and coffee they ate a little punnet of strawberries in the rear cockpit and finally sent the little chip-basket flying over the side with the stalks and stems.

'Just a drop of brandy, Lily. And then I'm going to tuck you up for the night.'

'Oh, I couldn't possibly sleep. I couldn't dream of it. I'm far, far too excited,' answered Mrs. Beanlands.

'No, I shall take the first watch and then you can take the second, if I can be spared,' said Shap firmly. 'I've got to make some observations of stars fairly soon.'

Wreaks shifted himself in his seat. He was feeling more tired than he expected and more bored. Behind him he could see a glimmer of light in the rear cockpit. For a little while his mind wandered and he thought of Burnaby. He remembered the engineer's shaking hand, shaking with whisky, and his big forehead. He was Burnaby's chum in the early days before he became a famous designer and he had become Burnaby's test pilot afterwards. It had been bad for his nerves. It wasn't bad at first, but after 1925 he had got a hunch that old Burnaby was trying to kill him. 'He never was the same to me after I lost my eye. That's a funny thing to change a man. But he was never the same.' But old Burnaby was killed himself now. 'If one lives long enough one sees anything happen. Every possible combination comes to pass in time. Given infinite time seven monkeys typing at random will type the *Encyclopedia Brittanica*.

'My hat, what a dotty joy-ride this is,' he reflected suddenly. 'If we come in for a strong head-wind in Asia, hell only knows where we shall run out of petrol. But I guess I can last out as long as the tanks provided that we don't bump into any of those beastly mountains.'

The dashboard light went out in the rear cockpit. It certainly was like travelling wagons-lits when all was said and done, reflected Lily. She must speak to dear Mr. Wreaks before she went to sleep.

'Only, of course, I shan't be able to sleep for excitement.' She yawned, and the wind tore at the top of her weary widowed head.

'Wilmot.'

'Lily, darling.'

For the moment she felt suspicious and resentful. Wilmot mustn't go too far. Then she remembered suddenly that they were comrades on the great adventure.

'Lily, darling Lily. All my life seems to have been a preparation leading to this. The most exciting, the most miraculous night of my life, transcending love and war, and all rendered possible by you, you who make it all worth while. That's what I am feeling.' Shap gave a surprising warm rich and gentle laugh at the end of this speech. 'If only I don't feel too terribly flat in the morning.'

Mrs. Beanlands took hold of his gloved hand and drew it to her. She was quite overcome by what Wilmot had said. For a moment or two they disputed which should kiss the other's gloved hand. Then Shap turned in his seat and putting his hand on the leather-covered bosom of the lady, pressed his lips to hers. Gently he tucked her up.

'Good night, sweetheart. Good night.'

'Good night, dear comrade. I feel so safe with you.'

To make certain of making each other hear they had to whisper these soft nothings into the respective mouthpieces of their telephones, which involved turning their heads away from each other as they spoke.

For Jimmy the night grew stale and sickly, and he sat solidly for three hours, but after that he began to feel himself slip every little while. He blinked his eye fast and looked at the lighted dash and all the luminous dials in front of him. First he read them one after another in a slow circle anti-clockwise, then he read them in the reverse order. Hell, he was slipping again.

He moved, shook his shoulders, and reached for the thermos of black coffee. The bitterness roused him to wakefulness and he remembered the gleaming tramlines, the wet streets, the lorries under the bridge, near Camden Town, and the traffic moving forward in a confused mass. His car had skidded as he braked violently, and the Ford lorry turned sharply in on him with an absurdly late outflung driver's hand. Glass fell in ringing splinters on the pavement. A tram pulled up short to avoid him. A policeman appeared. He mustn't let the Bobby smell his breath or he would never get a job again, had been his thought as he remained seated in his car answering questions rather stiffly.

The bubble wavered, and he pressed the stick quickly, too quickly, to one side. Presently he would begin to remind himself of McCudden and tell himself stories of all the great pilots he had known.

Just behind him Shap sat perfectly awake and self-possessed. For some hours he let his mind play on all the possibilities of the flight. At their present rate there was quite a chance that they would succeed in reaching Hong-Kong. He saw himself in the Club with Lily, being given a lunch in her honour. It would be *her* flight, *her* aeroplane, *her* fame, and so her gratitude would embrace him. If they once made a success of it he knew that he would be sure of her. Rich, generous and, in spite of her propriety, amorous, she was bound to marry him if he played his cards properly.

Shap smiled wearily. There was no reason to be nasty about it. They would suit each other. A widow of forty has advantages and a girl of twenty has drawbacks. . . . But to get back to brass tacks.

A blast of air struck him on the cheek and he leant forward and screamed wildly: 'Wreaks! Hi, Wreaks! Wake up!' The machine rocked violently and the wind in his face vanished.

'I say, old man, hadn't you better take her up a bit higher. Just in case you know. . . .'

'That's all right. That's my look-out. I let her skid a bit just now, but the bubble's rather hard to see in this light.'

Shap threw himself into conversation. At all events the pilot had to be kept awake. But Jimmy Wreaks would not answer. Shap's voice ringing in his ears exasperated him. It was queer how he had put on rudder unconsciously. He could only think that he must have dozed a little and pushed out one leg and drawn the other in without thinking what he was doing. He shook himself and looked about him. There was a lighter patch of sky in the east, but it couldn't be the dawn. 'I guess it's the moon. That will wake me up a bit when it rises. The sky is light enough in all conscience.'

He looked at the instruments in turn, then put his hand in his pocket and pulled out a brandy flask and gulped a big mouthful. The brandy burned him, it warmed him, he felt its glowing fingers run all through him caressing his numb body. It was fine. But this infernal fellow was still jabbering in his ear.

'How are you feeling, old chap? Will you give the air-speed reading?'

Wreaks groaned with annoyance and pulled out the connection of his telephone. The vast roar of the engine immediately replaced the insistent voice of the navigator.

'That's got rid of him for a bit,' he thought. Shap remained in ignorance of what had happened and went on talking and asking questions to which he got no reply. In a little while he was vowing vengeance secretly, but the explanation of the pilot's silence did not occur to him. The moon rose, and an hour later a grey crack was opening on the horizon. Half an hour later the dawn was breaking in the first pinks and pearl grey with a touch of gold. The stars had grown pale and disappeared. Below the earth was hidden and a pearly white sheet stretched as far as the eye could see. They appeared to be flying over a vast waveless sheet of water.

'I make out that we are somewhere in the heart

of Russia,' Shap said to himself. 'But can we have drifted north to Lake Ladoga? We must have done, and I can't get any answer out of that lunatic.'

Jimmy felt singularly happy and at peace with all the world. He wasn't tired or sleepy any longer and looked about him cheerily. At last the sun's rim appeared over the horizon and blinded him, and he hastily pulled out the cork with which he had plugged up the end of his telephone and connected it up so that he could hear what Shap had to say, and shouted:

'Good morning, Commander. Will you please note the time by the chronometer and give me our approximate longitude?'

'What's been the matter with you, eh? I'm glad you've found your voice again,' grumbled Shap angrily.

Jimmy burst into uncontrolled guffaws. 'I say I am sorry. I ought to have warned you. I disconnected my headphones in order to listen to the engine. I thought I heard something funny about it, but it was quite all right.'

'Oh, that's all right, Wreaks. No harm done. Why, we must be in longitude thirty-six. We've done marvellously.'

The two men were on good terms again. Shap thought: 'If only I could have a wash and a cigarette, I should feel all right for another twenty-four hours.' A mouthful of neat whisky cheered him.

Looking down he saw that what he had taken for water was a ground mist which vanished as he watched. It was lucky he had not spoken about it and given himself away.

Half an hour later Lily Beanlands woke up and looked about her. The sun falling directly into her eyes had woken her. She blinked. For a minute everything was red and black while her dream of a vast cascade of water, of Niagara Falls in which Alfred, her husband, was being washed away, haunted her. She moved and seeing Wilmot sitting beside her, she smiled at him. The roar of Niagara was the roaring of the engine. When she looked over the side of the cockpit, Russia seemed to her like a newly varnished toy which had only just been made. Below her she saw a rolling hill, a scattered forest of birch trees with open glades, which ran down to a wide uncultivated heath, where the birches were few and a great peat bog opened before her with regular squares and oblongs of cut peat with water lying in each and the turves standing beside them in cubical brown stacks. There was a light railway running through the forest to carry them away.

A screen of firs and birches cut off the heath, and they crossed a narrow road with two lodges by a park wall. Beyond, in the park, was a ruined house and farther on a hamlet with a green-roofed church with a blue cupola. There were goats grazing round the church. One of them was perched on the broken wall of brick which ran round the church. Then came more birch trees and waste land and peat cutting, and the links of a river winding among fields. And then more birch trees and more rivers and stacks of peat.

Wreaks was waving his arm and pointing: on the horizon to the south-east there was something gold and white glittering in the sunlight. The aeroplane banked suddenly in a steep turn towards it and she plugged in.

'Moscow.'

'Moscow! Are we going to fly over Moscow?' Over the Kremlin, where those dreadful Commissars plot to do away with rich people.

'They won't shoot at us, will they?' she asked anxiously. Wreaks laughed, a deep hearty laugh, and she felt reassured. Her fears of Bolshevism, and of Russia, subsided as the spectacle of Moscow unfolded itself.

From a distance the city seemed a cluster of white points, each tipped with gold, but as they drew closer the whole city, the expanse of houses and gardens, became dominated by an immense white building crowned with an enormous golden dome. The huge compact cathedral was the heart of Moscow: it seemed almost the whole of it, and only as they came closer could she make out in detail the Kremlin: a vast palace bordering the river beside the bridge, and surrounded by a jumble of domes and cupolas, and towers of lesser buildings with courtyards between them. She could see a piece of the wall running round it and a square on the other side, and then the town spreading out dingily into a great expanse beyond.

They were almost too high to notice the people in the streets, or to see if they stopped to look up at them. Beyond Moscow there were railway lines and huge fields of greeny yellow rye, and lines of pollard willows, a lake by a factory and a windmill on a piece of rising ground.

They had breakfast. The wonderful, marvellous experience of seeing Moscow from the air had delayed it, and they drank the hot coffee and ate the ham sandwiches and talked for some time enthusiastically about Moscow and about their flight.

When their powers of conversation were exhausted, Lily Beanlands got out her diary and her fountain pen and set to work.

'*The greatest adventure of my life*,' she headed it and spent two happy hours in composition.

'How wonderful it will seem of me to have written

it in the air actually before the end of our adventure, not yet knowing whether we shall fail or triumph,' she thought.

'*I begin to believe that we shall break the record*,' she wrote. '*That record which has been the object of our thoughts for months*.' The business about the record was, she remembered, rather a complicated one. She must ask Wilmot about it later. She always forgot.

Jimmy turned and waved his hand. Wilmot tapped her elbow.

The Volga!

'Oh, Wilmot! The Volga. How wonderful. How marvellous. How romantic. The Volga! Just think, the Volga!'

Wreaks smiled savagely as these raptures reached him.

'What the hell does the woman think happens if you make a bee-line across Europe?' he said to himself. 'You must get somewhere if you burn all this petrol.'

The river itself was, when they looked at it, extremely fine. It was very wide, and they could see a steamer going up and another coming down. And there were three islands in a row.

'South of Kazan,' announced Shap. 'We've come a good way south of our route you know. In three or four hours we ought to get to the Urals.'

Mrs. Beanlands went back to her log and began describing the Volga.

'*I almost thought of asking Jimmy to stop the engine and glide down in the hope that we should hear a snatch of the boat-song wafted up to us. But such nonsense must not be allowed to come between us and our great objective.*'

There was no longer anything they could do. It had become boring looking at Russia. Lily and Wilmot connected up their telephones and talked for a couple of hours brightly about the French coast, discussing each little town between Marseilles and Mentone all the way along the Riviera, each with its hotels and casinos, when they had each been there, what local inhabitants they had met, the prices they had paid, the weather they had enjoyed and the awful occasions when they had been ill abroad and had to call in a French doctor.

They no longer noticed how time went and had forgotten where they were.

'We're in sight of the Urals. We crossed a railway about five minutes ago. I want you to spot our exact position.'

Shap became busy. 'We've not done quite so well,' he announced.

'Asia!' cried Lily. 'We're crossing into Asia!' To their surprise the Urals looked quite a fine range of mountains. A big peak stood up to the south, and they bumped a bit. But after a quarter of an hour Asia became very much like Europe, and after a technical conversation Shap returned to discuss the Éden Roc hotel at Antibes. Talking of hotels made them hungry and they munched chocolate and malted milk tablets. Wreaks joined in and ate chocolate and malted milk himself. Then he drank a little brandy. He was beginning to ache in different places and suffer from pins and needles.

They flew over a lake and identified it, and slowly the hours dragged by. The sun sank low; at four-thirty, Greenwich time, it set.

'We can't be far from Akmolinsk,' said Shap.

'There are two serious dangers now,' announced Wreaks suddenly in ringing tones. 'The first is that a northerly wind should have been drifting us down to Kizyl Rai and that we should hit it. That isn't very likely. The other is that I should run into the Tarbagata or the Narym Mountains before dawn. Will you please check for wind drift by dropping a flare?'

It was obvious even to Lily that Wreaks was seriously worried because they had not identified their position before darkness fell.

'The only thing which may save us is the moon. Only I don't know when it rises.'

As Wreaks betrayed anxiety, Shap became propitiatory and deferential and put forward consoling suggestions with the utmost tact. But Jimmy was not to be made easy in his mind and kept Shap busy making observations again and again, and made him read out his calculations to him.

He was torn between the desire to push on as fast as possible (in which lay their only chance of reaching Hong-Kong) and a terror of arriving while it was still dark in the vicinity of mountains 14,000 feet or more high. As time went on it became clear that he was becoming definitely nervous. The earth was invisible, not a light showed on it, but after five hours the sky grew paler ahead of them. Half an hour later the moon rose, revealing the peaks of a great mountain range.

'Those must be the Narym Mountains. The Altai,' said Shap.

'Well, it has come out just in time. I shan't bump into them now.'

The moon rose higher and the mountains showed black and surprisingly clear. Suddenly another range appeared closer to them on their right. 'That's splendid!' shouted Jimmy. 'Just what we ought to find.'

A bump struck them, and the machine rocked violently. Another bump. Flying became a new and difficult art, and Wreaks had to put his head inside the cockpit and watch the illuminated dash and winking little green and red lights of the turn indicator.

The mountains were becoming near and awe-inspiring, and Wreaks banked the machine and swung off on a north-easterly compass course.

'Here's the lake, Jimmy,' said Shap, delighted with the good news.

The soft moonlight gleamed over an unmistakable stretch of water. Jimmy looked out at the great mountain ranges towards which he was flying, shutting him in ahead and on his right. They were not black in the moonlight but all sorts of subdued colours, purple, violet, brown and dusky blue with dull silvery ribs of glacier shining softly in the yellow moonlight, and while the machine rocked, fighting the wind which blew off them, he licked his lips and stared.

'That's what I came for,' he whispered to himself. 'My God, I'm not too old yet. This is the lake and we keep straight over it until we spot the Irtysh. Damn it all, I wish Donald was here, or somebody that understood. It would have just sent him crazy.'

Donald had been an observer of Jimmy's. He had been dead thirteen years.

'If there were any clouds now, or fog, we should be dead men.'

The mountains drew together and overhung them. The lake narrowed and the silvery bar of the river stretched away between the shadows of the mountains.

Jimmy grunted an assent as Shap called out: 'The Irtysh!' but his heart sang: 'The Irtysh. I've found the Black Irtysh in the dark and here comes the dawn in a glory of fire over the snows of the Altai. At last I'm living again. It's damn fine. It's grand.'

But instead of such words he answered: 'Give me the compass course for the river. I'll fly by compass for a bit, and then come back to it so you can estimate our drift.'

The machine was needing a great deal of careful flying. The great mountain peaks drew close and their progress was slow.

'It's a head-wind!' The mountains were changing colour. On the left they were shadows of blue, hanging in screens, range behind range, like the wings and scenery running off the stage. But on the right they had been touched by the first rays of the sun and were solid, yellow, golden, green and veined with black. The sun blazed up over Eastern Turkestan, the wind backed to the north, and for a time they made more progress.

Two hours after dawn, as they passed over the Dzungarian uplands, just to the north of Bogda-ola, which rose to a height of 22,000 feet in a sheer cliff, they ran into a head-wind. It was bumpy and violent, and for a time Wreaks had his hands full. But far worse than the bumps was the fact that the ground speed fell off noticeably.

An hour later, when they had left Bogda-ola behind them, they began to climb steadily, and Wreaks swung the machine due south. 'Here we go over the pass,' explained Shap, but Lily didn't like the pass, though, of course, the mountains were simply titanic. But the pass was too bumpy altogether until she saw the earth drop away into a deep valley. Jimmy skirted the valley and began to take the machine down. They passed over a mud town. 'There is Hami, and ahead of us we should see the Pe-shan.' The headwind was awful.

'I'll go as low as I can and see if I can get along a bit faster,' said Jimmy. For the next hour they flew very low down, rocking and bumping violently in the wind.

The land was a broken country of desert. Rocks of all shapes and sizes, from pebbles to haystacks, were scattered thickly over a flattish plain, which became broken up into a hilly region as they approached the foothills of a mountain range, behind which, in the south, Wreaks could catch sight of the snow-capped range of the Nan-shan.

Suddenly a few drops of oil appeared on the little windscreen in front of him, and before his mind could grasp what was happening a stream of oil was being sprayed back from under the engine cowling over his face and helmet. He ducked his head instinctively, but he could not avoid the shower of oil which covered his goggles and blinded him. Instinctively he shut the throttle and switched off the engine and then, driven desperate by the oil, banked the machine and held its nose up with top rudder, sideslipping wildly into wind, and pushing his goggles off

as he did so, to see with his one eye. The rocks rushed at them from the tilted wing. Rocks, rocks, rocks. Nothing but rocks, and a stretch where large pebbles lay thickly in a blue and white bed at the bottom of a dry water-course, overhung by low bluffs of earth.

Wreaks no sooner saw this spot than he put the nose of the machine down and turned her quickly on the glide, and then pulling the nose sharply up, sideslipped right down on to the rocky edge of the bluff. The rocks rushed up into Lily Beanlands' face, the rush of wind tore her face as they dropped. As they almost touched the cliff's edge, Wreaks checked the slip sharply and glided down on to the bed of the stream. The passengers behind him lurched each way as he swish-tailed violently, slowing the machine until he knew that it must crash. At the last moment Wreaks put the stick back a bit more—a bit more, and deliberately stalled four feet above the earth. Bounce! Crash! They had hit one of the bigger boulders ahead, and the tail of the machine rose in the air, the left side of the undercarriage collapsed, the wing-tip caught in the stones and splintered and tore. All was suddenly still, in a state of perfect repose. Everything had been quiet; it seemed for a very long while, ever since the engine had been switched off.

In the quietness they could hear Shap swearing. He had tried to jump clear and had been jerked back by his headphones. Wreaks was in pain. His left foot was trapped and twisted. He could not extricate it from between the rudder bar, which had been pushed up, and a strut of the undercarriage which had come up through the fuselage. Lily Beanlands was very collected.

'We ought to get out quickly in case the machine should catch fire.' After saying this she detached her telephone connection and climbed out unaided, on the right side of the machine, from which she had to jump some way down to the ground. Shap had already jumped out on the left. Wreaks remained immovable, twisting his crushed foot laboriously. At last he got it free, unstrapped his belt, disconnected his telephone, and pulled himself up out of the cockpit with his hands. Then he slid gently over the side of the fuselage.

The three of them stood in front of the machine and looked at it.

'Oil-pipe bust,' said Wreaks.

The nose of the aeroplane was lying on the ground, the left-hand side of the undercarriage had telescoped up, and the left wing was bent back and shattered at the tip. Petrol was dripping from a buckled tank in the left wing, and all the front of the machine glistened green-bronze with oil. It did not occur to any of the three to begin to do anything. Commander Shap and Mrs. Beanlands stood huddled together, surveying the wreckage. Jimmy Wreaks sat down on the ground, and began to untie the laces of the boot on his crushed foot. At intervals Shap walked round the wreck and came away from it again.

Then he climbed up the steep bluff or cliff of earth which was the bank of the dry river in which they had come down. When he reached the top he called to Mrs. Beanlands.

'Come up, will you, Lily? You can see a lot of the country here. Will you bring my field-glasses with you?'

Mrs. Beanlands set off; she climbed and slipped on the friable, shaly, dry clay, and when she was three-quarters of the way up the almost vertical bank, she got stuck and called to Wilmot Shap to help her. Jimmy looked up at the shaky figure, making uncertain movements, and grinned pityingly at her embarrassment.

After Shap had hauled her up, they did not come back for some time, and Jimmy dozed away the worst of the sickening pain.

Shap was speaking. 'My word, it was hot up there moving about.' Wreaks looked at the perspiring faces and listened.

'It's real desert. There's hardly any vegetation except a prickly sort of whin and a few patches of stonecrop. Otherwise it's all stones and rocks. . . . We didn't see any other possible landing-place. We were lucky to get down here. And now we'll have lunch and consider plans afterwards, when we're all more recovered.'

They ate three rather stale sandwiches, each with varying degrees of enjoyment, and then munched some chocolate, after which Jimmy dozed off again like a drugged man. Mrs. Beanlands took the rest of the food and put it away in the cockpit, and Shap climbed once more up the bluff with a map in his hand and sat in the shade of a big rock, smoking his pipe. Wreaks, who was a cigarette smoker, had come without any. Shap did not offer him his pipe tobacco.

Long shadows fell from every stone; dusk gathered in the distances; the wind dropped and a chill fell on the wrecked voyagers. Wreaks sat cross-legged in pain, fingering the swollen instep and ankle, while Shap moved to and fro, hunting through the 'plane hoping to find something useful. He brought out the food. There was very little left: a parcel or two of sandwiches, an untouched thermos of black coffee and another of hot milk, half a pound of nut-milk chocolate, a tube of Horlick's tablets.

Mrs. Beanlands, who had slipped off, came back, having discovered a tiny runnel of water on the opposite side of the river-bed. She went back to it with an empty thermos and filled it with water.

'I'm going to make some malted milk,' she announced. 'What can I burn, Mr. Wreaks?'

'Tear off a bit of that wing fabric,' he suggested. 'But bring it right away from the 'plane or we shall have the whole thing in a blaze.'

The darkness seemed to fall faster for the little flame. Lily Beanlands had to heat the water a cupful at a time, in the metal tops of the thermos flasks. She held them in a pair of pliers she took out of the tool locker.

'Here you are, Jimmy, I am so sorry about your poor foot. But isn't it wonderful? To be alive, I mean.'

Wreaks was grateful for the hot malted milk and felt that it had done him good, but he was too exhausted to speak and in too much pain. Moreover, he had not even yet finished cursing himself for letting the accident catch him when he was flying so low. 'If I had had 500 feet in hand I could have put her down somewhere safely and have mended the oil-pipe. But now we are done. Finish. And to be stranded with such a pair of ghastly love-birds. Poor old girl, I suppose it's not her fault, but I wish the family had kept her under restraint.'

He sat rubbing the strained ligaments and cursing himself silently until sleep swiftly came, and his head dropping on to his arms, he collapsed, fast asleep, pillowed on some scattered stones.

He was woken by Shap shaking him by the arm.

'Hey, what's that?' he said fiercely, quarrelsome in his sleep and then blinking his one eye open upon the world. The sun was shining brilliantly, already high up in a cloudless blue sky.

'She wouldn't let me wake you before, but it's time we were moving, old boy. You and I have got to have a council of war.'

Jimmy spat. Then he stood up, and a stab of pain reminded him of his ankle. A small fire was smoking a few yards from the wrecked aeroplane and the smoke rose in a thin column straight up in the air.

'No wind,' Wreaks noted automatically. But

what did the wind matter? That 'plane would never fly again.

'Look here, Wreaks,' said Shap in a low voice. 'I'm responsible for Mrs. Beanlands' safety. We've got to find some natives. We've got to leave you here until we can send for you, because of your foot.'

'That's all right,' said Jimmy, putting his hand over his mouth and yawning.

'I want to start at once. You realise that I must take what's left of the food, don't you? Also one of the compasses, although it's so heavy.'

'Come and have a cup of malted milk, Jimmy,' called Mrs. Beanlands, climbing out from the cock-pit of the aeroplane. 'I wouldn't let Wilmot wake you before. Aren't you grateful? You were in such a sound sleep. You were really, and you deserved it. The more I have been thinking over our descent, the more I am convinced that we all owe our lives to you.'

Wreaks took the thermos top in his handkerchief and lifted it to his lips.

'Have you had your breakfast, Mrs. Beanlands?'

he asked, feeling strangely solicitous for this woman's welfare. 'I'm afraid I've been precious little use.'

'We've had ours. There are two sandwiches for your breakfast as well. We've each had two sandwiches. Wilmot has worked out that we must be really quite close to China.' She laughed. 'So we are going to go off, leaving you, and find some Chinese.'

Wreaks laughed, and took the two sandwiches from her and wrapped them up in his handkerchief.

'Wilmot is desperately anxious to set off at once. Of course, we can't tell how far we may have to walk to get help.'

Wreaks sat down and sipped the malted milk meditatively. It was delicious. He was surprised that Mrs. Beanlands should turn out so well in an emergency.

'Are you ready to start, Lily?' called Shap. 'We want to get off before the heat of the day.'

'I'm leaving you one of the empty thermos flasks; it will do to carry water in if you can get as far as the stream with your poor foot,' said Lily.

Wreaks struggled to his feet and hopped up to her.

'I should like to say I think you are a very plucky woman. You've been very kind. . . . It has been a great pleasure. . . . I wish I had put up a better show.' They took each other's hands rather emotionally.

'Well, till to-morrow. I hope we shall be able to send for you to-night—but if not, then to-morrow.'

'Good-bye.'

'Good-bye.'

'Good luck. Don't overdo the first day's march if you can't find any natives.'

'We shall be all right, old chap.'

'Good-bye.'

They crossed the bed of the river and began to climb the opposite bank, picking their way carefully and moving slowly and laboriously. At the top they turned to wave. They were black figures standing against the sun. Jimmy pulled himself up to attention and gave a military salute. Then they were gone.

'Now I settle down and make myself cosy,' he said

to himself. He finished the last drop of the malted milk and taking the sandwiches out of his pocket hopped with them in his hand to the aeroplane.

'She wasn't a bad woman. I always knew she had guts, only she was a damned fool to want to come on this trip.'

Shap had taken the map for this section with him, and Jimmy regretted he had not discussed their position with him before he left. Perhaps it was marked in the log. His own belief was that they were about fifty or a hundred miles north of a line connecting An-hsi-chow and Su-chow. His ankle unfortunately prevented him from climbing up on the bluff and viewing the country. All he could see was the bed of the dry water-course in which the 'plane lay, and the cliff, or wall of earth, which bounded it in the other side. He was hungry and the sun was hot. 'When shall I eat the first sandwich?' he asked himself, looking at the little parcel in his hand.

'To-night, at nine o'clock, I will eat it and to-morrow night I will eat the second.' But thinking of time, as a hungry man must, reminded him that he should wind the chronometer in case it should run down. His wrist watch had stopped; he had forgotten it the previous night. He hopped along the side of the fuselage to the rear cockpit, balancing himself by gripping the edge. Then laying his precious sandwiches on the fuselage, he drew himself up with difficulty and seated himself in Shap's seat. First he put away the sandwiches in a pigeon-hole in the dash, then he wound the chronometer, which was ticking. It read 12.48, and for a moment he was puzzled, but he soon realised that it was A.M. That was by English summer-time; by local (perhaps Indian) time it must have been about seven o'clock in the morning.

He glanced at the maps which were left and picked up Shap's sextant. On Mrs. Beanlands' seat there were lying her heavy fur coat, her flying helmet and goggles, and her electrically heated flying-suit. In the pocket at the back of Shap's seat was a notebook with what she had written of the LOG OF THE WAYZGOOSE, and stuck among its pages two unposted addressed letters which she must have written on the journey. There was a small parcel of some of her clothes.

Jimmy decided to make an inventory of useful objects sometime later in the day. But, at the moment, what did it matter what he did or did not do? He was alone, absolutely alone, and had to wait fourteen hours before he ate a sandwich. Until then he could pass the time as he liked.

Scruples held him back from reading Mrs. Beanlands' diary of the flight, though he was certain that it would amuse him. He laid it unopened in the pigeon-hole on top of the sandwiches, telling himself that he must remember to take it and her letters with him when the Chinese, or Mongolians, or Tibetans, arrived to fetch him, if they ever did. It might easily take Shap three days before he reached a village, or fell in with a shepherd. The shepherd would take him and Mrs. Beanlands to the headquarters of the tribe; the headman might take them on to the nearest Chinese official so that an expedition to rescue him would probably not set out till the fourth or fifth day. It might take as much as two days to reach him, even for mounted men. Thus, his rescue might not take place for a week, but if nine days went by he would know that there was no hope.

'On the other hand, it may be to-morrow,' he said aloud, and laughed.

'There is one great consolation: thank God, I haven't got a broken leg, or she would have stayed here to nurse me. Hoo! Hoo! Think of that! Think of being left with a woman without a bite of food for a week or a fortnight! Fancy offering to let her eat me, or else making up my mind to eat her! One couldn't toss up for a thing like that with a woman.'

Such thoughts put Jimmy in a good humour and made him forget his hunger for a little while. But he grew thirsty.

'I'll go and look at the spring or whatever it is, where she found water.'

He climbed out, and after unscrewing one of the undercarriage struts to serve as a staff to support himself, he hobbled across the bed of the water-course, or *wady*, as he called it, from his experience of Arabia. The ground was thickly strewn with round pebbles and cobble stones, interspersed with a few larger boulders. The bed of the *wady* was perhaps a hundred yards across. The aeroplane had crashed on the left-hand northern side of it, which Wreaks had chosen at the last moment as the boulders were fewer there. On the far side was a little trickle of water running among the stones, expanded here and there in its course into shallow stagnant puddles, marked by a clump of reeds or coarse grass. On the bed of the *wady* itself there was no vegetation growing among the white and blue polished pebbles. Wreaks scooped up water to wash his hands and face, then he filled the empty thermos with water and drank his fill, and then made a little pit in the bed of the trickle of water and held his injured foot in it.

The water was pleasant and refreshing, though not very cold. It tasted of iron. 'It's handy,' he said. 'But what a place to crash!'

When he turned and saw the machine lying in a

river-bed among so many broken boulders and big rocks, he marvelled how he had got down without worse damage.

There were no traces of life at the pool; no foot-prints of beasts or birds. 'There must be other water not far off that they prefer,' he argued. 'I shall have to shoot something for supper. I've got my pistol.'

He had left it in the front cockpit of the aeroplane, and a sudden fear that Shap had taken it assailed him, and he began to hobble back after he had filled up the thermos flask again.

How lonely the dry river-bed with its loosely cobbled floor and the white wings lying broken under the sunshine of Mongolia! How lonely! How silent to ears jaded by the roar of engines never ceasing day or night! How silent! Solitude, loneli-ness, emptiness, silence—Wreaks had experienced these often enough when planing down with a shut throttle from a height of 20,000 feet above the earth, through a desert of cloud forms or phan-tom Polar sea. At such times he would hear nothing but the *whick*, *whick*, *whick* of the slowly spinning airscrew and would see no living thing in the desert about him unless, perchance, it were the moving phantom of himself: his shadow.

But he was not at the mercy of the desert of the sky. He was free, happy as a living bird, full of mastery. With a movement of his thumb he could make the empty spaces echo and in ten minutes he could descend gently among the 'planes which circled about the grassy aerodrome. If he were pressed for time he could put the machine in a spin and come down as fast as the angels falling out of heaven, watching the earth appear through the clouds and open out to him while it revolved like a roulette wheel slowly coming to rest. In a minute he could be listening to empty-headed laughter and a jazz record on the gramophone.

But in this desert of the earth he moped feebly, seeking shade by lying under the monoplane's broken wing and rousing himself only to look at the fractured steel of the undercarriage.

Five pebbles were balanced on the dead-white

scarred back of a hand. The wrist flicked and four were caught in the palm. But the game of knucklebones is played the other way: thrown up from the palm and balanced on the back of the hand. Three stayed and two rolled off. Two stayed and three fell. Four stayed and one fell. One remained, balanced alone, and four were scattered. . . . But at all events they clinked together making a sound to break the monotony of hunger.

If he could not take a siesta, he could lie with his eye tightly shut; if he could not forget food, he could tighten his belt. He could make a target of a pebble balanced on a rock and sit in the shade and throw others to knock it off.

For the last hour before sunset he sat and massaged his foot, resolving to spend the whole of the next morning in the same dismal occupation, since as soon as the inflammation went down he would be able to move about and find something to eat. He could not climb the bluff until his foot was better, and the thought came to him that there might be herds of sheep, or, who knows, yaks, grazing within sight on that stony land, or a line of Bactrian camels crossing the desert laden with rhubarb, within a mile of where he lay starving. At last the sun began to set and he climbed up into the cockpit where he had laid his sandwiches. It was only two minutes to three by the chronometer. The sun set at twenty past nine in England, and he decided that he would go by local time for his meals. Otherwise he would have to keep himself awake at night and eat in the dark.

He took out one sandwich and ate it very slowly, crumb by crumb, washing it down with a pint or so of water. The other sandwich he put away, though he was ravenously hungry after his meal, and as he drew on his airman's leather suit and the fleece-lined thigh boots, the fur gauntlets and the fur-lined hat, it seemed to him that he never would be able to go to sleep. But he was still weary after his flight and exhaustion gained the victory over hunger. After half an hour he was peacefully asleep, his last thought being a hope that he would be awakened by the crunch of footsteps on the loose stones.

The sun was hot upon him; he was drenched in sweat and his head ached. It was late, and he had been sleeping for hours in his thick fur-lined leather suit. The stones near him were hot to the touch when he sat up. He felt ill and faint with hunger, and staggering on to his feet hobbled painfully to the 'plane, pulled the sandwich out of its hiding-place and looked at it.

'I daresay a rescue party will be here by lunch-time with gallons of hot bovril,' he said to himself and took a bite. Angrily and reluctantly he ate the two slices of desiccated bread and the withered slice of tongue that curled black and greasy between their roughness. A crumb fell, and when he had finished he went down on hands and knees to pick over the stones until it was retrieved.

That day was terrible. His hunger increased. He sipped water continually but without quenching his thirst, and his heaviness and headache were so great that he thought a sunstroke could be the only cause. But worse than all physical pains was the torture of anticipation. At every moment he was looking up quickly, thinking to see mounted figures appear on the opposite bank of the river and wave to him. He would wave back and they would descend, leaning back on their horses' haunches at a spot about half a mile away, where the slope was not so steep. He looked towards it with his hawk's eye, and the stone wavered in a mist of heat under the sun.

His tongue was furry and his throat was sore. He struggled with difficulty to the runnel of water, and, never having been ill before in his life, became convinced that he was dying.

'I do believe that I am going to croak. I do honestly,' he said aloud in a strange voice that evening, as he sat massaging the purple flesh of his bruised ankle and instep, and he determined to resort to his last hope in the most desperate of emergencies: his brandy flask which he had hidden so that he should be out of the way of temptation.

For a moment or two he thought that he would not be able to pull himself up by the struts into the cockpit, for his head spun and his strength seemed to have gone. But he pulled and struggled and his heavy body seemed suddenly to be released by something that had been holding it down.

He took a gulp of brandy while he sat in the cockpit, then, feeling restored, climbed out. His head still ached, and his stomach whined for food, but his weakness was gone. Before drinking again he pulled on his airman's clothes and went to lie down in the bed he had made of Mrs. Beanlands' fur coat and the seats of the cushions, under the broken wing. As he crawled into this kennel the effort made him sweat violently and his head felt as though it were splitting. Another pull at the brandy flask stopped him from actually crying out with the pain. The brandy ran like fire down his arms; it glowed deliciously in his stomach and crept in a fiery embrace round to the small of his back, but it was the taste of it on his tongue which delighted him beyond everything. It was so delicious a flavour that he reflected bitterly on the cruel fate which allowed him to have such an agonising pain in his head to distract him while he was drinking it. He sipped again, and then drank a great gulp. It was nectar; the smell of it tickled his nostrils; the volatile spirit was inhaled into his lungs. He drank another mouthful and his headache was gone. He lay disembodied, almost swooning in bliss, savouring the brandy, not disturbed by the softly swaying earth that rolled beneath him and slipped away from him ever so gently.

'Earth-pockets. There are earth-pockets,' he said, delighted at the new thought. 'But I don't care. I'm so damned stable. It's the hot days and the cold nights: contractions, expansions. . . .'

Lifting the flask to his lips, he drained it of the last drop. The contractions and expansions swayed him, and then suddenly the earth beneath him began to move round and round like a top, and he felt himself moving with it.

'A spin. I'm spinning. Opposite rudder. I haven't been drunk like this since I was a boy, and on less than half a bottle of brandy! I didn't know it was possible. Spin again. I won't! I won't!'

As his will hardened he felt himself oscillate like the needle of a compass; then he was lying perfectly still in bed. His will relaxed and he felt himself begin to turn again, but before he had done two turns he was asleep.

The light was fresh and innocent, and Wreaks looked out upon a jumbled floor of clean cobblestones and the far bank of the dry river throwing its shadow over him.

'It's early yet,' he said to himself. 'But I have slept well and am recovered.' The pangs of hunger had diminished, and his head was clear. Best of all, however, was that his ankle was much less swollen; indeed, it seemed to be quite well until he rose up and put his weight on it.

No sooner had he stood up than he lay down again, for there was nothing he could do during the day, except play knucklebones and fetch himself water from the runnel, and he was not anxious to start the day early. But before he composed himself to sleep again he pulled off his airman's clothing and his fur helmet. The air was warm already, and it would bring on another headache if he lay sweating wrapped up in furs. Sleep did not come easily, and he lay with his thoughts, not coloured either by bitterness or by affection, playing round the figure of his wife in England.

She had married him on his first leave after he had got his wings, during the war, in December 1916, and he thought with regret of the R.F.C. uniform. How fond he had been of his little forage cap with the tiny line of red piping! But he would not let his mind stray to the R.F.C. He would think of his wife.

She was never the same to him after he was so badly burnt; perhaps it would be truer to say that he was never the same to her. With most women it would not have made any difference: most women would have been proud of the cross they gave him when he was thought to be dying—but she never seemed proud of him, only numbed with horror. His temper was terrible for a time, he knew that, but it was the scars that upset her most. That was odd.

Directly he was able to pass a medical board he asked to be allowed to go out to France again, but he was sent as an instructor to Scotland instead. Daphne did not go with him. After his medical board she had said, astonished: 'Surely you're not going to fly again, Jimmy.' Nothing she had said or done, wounded him as much as that. She couldn't understand why he did.

Well, he had flown again; and then, of course, he had had that nasty crash in 1924 when he lost his eye. It was while he was at home convalescent that he found out that Daphne was having a love-affair with a schoolmaster. She begged him not to divorce her.

'I swear to be faithful to you, Jimmy. I swear to be a good wife.' Now if he didn't turn up; if he were to starve to death she would presume his death and marry the fellow. Daphne herself would never go up in a 'plane and was frightened for her own safety when he flew low over the house.

'You know low flying is dangerous, Jimmy. You ought to consider other people's feelings.' That was how she put it.

'But there have been worse marriages than ours,'

he reflected. 'We don't quarrel and we respect each other.' It is doubtful what he meant by this, but it was sincere, and perhaps it meant something.

He dozed, he slept; the sun rose higher; it passed the meridian. A little sound woke the sleeper, a faint buzz, a far-away hum, and on opening his eyes he beheld an exquisitely balanced little flying machine circling in figures of eight before his face. It was a fly, the first fly he had seen, the first living thing he had seen. On the previous day he had scanned the sky often, but he had not once seen a bird.

'Perhaps the next thing I shall see will be a 'plane,' he thought, watching the cruising fly. And suddenly a terrible idea jumped into his mind: that a 'plane might pass over him, or within a few miles of him, without seeing him; that, perhaps, they were already looking for him without success. There was a pistol in the 'plane which shot Very lights, but he wanted more than that: something which would mark the place for longer. He needed a beacon. Already he had crawled out from beneath the broken wing and was standing up looking about him, and anxiously he scanned the sky. A machine might come at any time. But whether the time of waiting proved short or long, a machine would certainly come looking for him in the end. Of that he felt certain.

'Think of all the people who sent out machines to search for Nobile,' he said to himself. 'I shall stay here until they come and I must build a beacon from where they can see it: on the top of the bluff.' Holding his strut as a staff he began to climb the sloping bank of earth and found his foot was better than he had supposed possible; it would bear his weight so long as he moved slowly, so that his fears of a broken bone in the instep were proved groundless. His foot was only bruised.

Climbing, however, was slow work, and the bluff crumbled quickly so that it was difficult to maintain a foothold. It was composed of dark earth, full of blackish shale: he had seen such a formation on the moors in Yorkshire and wondered for a moment whether here also it went with patches of surface coal.

When at last he had gained the top, he was rewarded by a wide view to the west, the north and the south. Only to the east was there higher broken ground with cliffs which must mark the foothills leading to those mountain ranges which he had seen capped with snow a moment before the oil-pipe broke. To the south-west he could trace the course of the river-bed descending into a broken country of rocks and little kopjes. But to the north and north-west it was flatter, and the land seemed to run in rocky terraces or ridges which faded out into a flatter, distant plain. This confirmed his general impression of the country when he was flying, but he had been too low down, fighting with a head-wind, to get an extensive view.

When he looked down into the river-bed he saw the wrecked machine lying at his feet and realised that it might easily be overlooked from the air. But since if any airman did see it, he would know what had happened, he must be careful, in building his beacon, to leave the fabric of the wings and elevator in position so that it should still be recognisable as a wrecked machine from the air. He must construct his beacon from the plywood and fabric of the fuselage, and from what spruce members he could remove from the wings, without spoiling their look.

After making his plans and sitting some time on the edge of the bluff he planted his strut on the site of his beacon and began the descent, often having to cling with his hands at the slippery wall of shale to prevent himself slipping and rolling to the bottom.

That day he made six ascents, and on each carried up a bundle for his beacon strapped upon his shoulders. But before he could begin he had to work for some time with his jack-knife, untying the fabric cover of the fuselage and unscrewing the panels of plywood, which had afterwards to be split and torn up into pieces of manageable size. In the execution of his work he became so absorbed that he forgot the hunger gnawing at his belly and the pain of his crushed foot and only paused for a moment, when he was tired out and trembling, to take a draught of water and to wipe away the sweat on his forehead. While he was still working with screwdriver and hammer, jack-knife and spanner at dismembering the fuselage, he saw that the shadows had grown long and that the sun was setting.

It was dusk when he came down after carrying up his last load and sat for a little while, too weary to put on his night-clothes, as his flying-suit had now become. After a little he roused himself, and, crawling into his kennel below the wing, he sat there with his head and shoulders pressing against the underside of the wing, massaging his foot. He was very hungry, but made up his mind that he would not think of food until after he had got his beacon built, which would take him the whole of the next day, for he could carry very little up with him at one time. His mind was so full of plans that sleep did not come easily: no sooner had one problem been solved, and a course of action decided on, than a new idea presented itself which he felt that he must debate in his own mind. Thus his thoughts raced, without control, in a sort of circular pattern, until at last the problems he set himself, and the ideas which assailed him, became irrelevant to his situation, and when at last he fell asleep it was with the conviction that he must remember to mark his grave on the map which he had decided to make in his log-book, and that he would call it *organic remains.*

The next morning the sun was high up when he awoke, but there was a gentle breeze which fluttered a piece of newspaper which he had left in the cockpit. He felt weak rather than excessively hungry, and took a large draught of water and two tablets of cascara from the bottle which he had slipped into his waistcoat pocket on the morning of the flight before setting out. Then he set promptly about the great work of loosening one of the petrol tanks in the wing, after draining all the petrol out of it into the lower tank. When at last he had got it out he carried it up on to the bluff empty, intending afterwards to carry petrol up in small quantities until he had enough stored away, not only to set his beacon blazing quickly, but also, to make a very great flare itself, if he should need to signal again after his bonfire had burnt itself out.

That was his principal work that day, interrupted only by forced rests when he was tired, and by the calls of nature, and by two or three visits to the runnel to refill his little brandy flask with water, for he had sacrificed the thermos to the task of carrying petrol. In climbing the bluff he always used the same way and soon left a transverse line across the face of the steep bank of earth and could balance himself securely as he climbed up, even when he had the empty tank on his shoulders, though he could not put it down to rest himself.

That evening he decided to improve his shelter under the broken wing, as the wind had risen and the weather had turned colder. Indeed, the wind seemed cold enough to bring snow with it, though it was June. Perhaps this was because the wind was blowing straight off the snow mountains he had seen and the elevation was 6000 feet.

The next morning he woke up feeling better in health than he had done since he had been there, and although he still limped when he walked, his foot did not ache whenever he let it touch the ground. He did not suffer from hunger at all, though he often stopped to drink water. During the morning he amused himself by looking over the engine and by repairing the oil-pipe which had caused all their trouble by coming adrift. It was an easy matter to screw it on again.

'Who knows,' he said to himself. 'There may be a chance of salving that engine, and it's worth a lot of money.'

After that he busied himself in taking off the rudder and the doors of the cockpits, intending to use these to build the walls of his little kennel or booth, the roof of which was the damaged wing.

In the afternoon he climbed again on to the bluff in order to have a look-out, as it occurred to him that perhaps a mounted party might be searching for him in the waste. As soon as he lifted his head over the edge of the bluff he caught sight of a big light-brown bird of prey, an eagle or a buzzard, which rose up from a big rock where it was perched and flew away.

He sat for some time, motionless, on the edge of the bluff, with his hands pressed down on the stones, staring at the bird until it was out of sight, his heart full of anger and savage envy that it should fly, and that he himself was bound to the earth, helpless. And even after the bird was gone he remained sitting there gazing at the sky and at the peaks of the snow mountains in the distance. While he was transfixed thus, an idea came to him, and suddenly he called out aloud: 'I must have a kite!' And tumbling over this thought came the second, that he must build himself a glider.

And without waiting to scan the plain for any rescue party which might be seeking him, he went down the bluff as fast as he could to look again at his wrecked aeroplane and plan in his mind how the glider was to be made. But, alas, what had seemed a possible and happy way of escape, when he was sitting on the bluff, showed itself as an absurd delusion when he was once more standing beside the machine. The wing of the aeroplane was far too thick and heavy to serve for a glider, and it would need taking entirely to pieces and rebuilding with planes, saws and chisels, with glue and dope and a whole armoury of carpenter's tools, not one of which

he had got. He had nothing of that sort indeed; only the tools for his engine: hammers and wrenches and screwdrivers. His only wood-working tool was his jack-knife, and he knew that he could not whittle a glider out of an aeroplane with that. He had never flown a glider, but that argument would not have deterred him if another, more powerful, had not presented itself.

'It would take me six months to build a glider with my knife, but I have no food, and unless I find food I cannot live more than a fortnight longer.'

When he had thus proved that it was not possible to make a glider he went back to his first idea, that he should make a kite.

'Anyone can make a kite,' he said to himself contemptuously. But it was some time before he could determine on its materials, for he could not find a piece of wood long enough and light enough for the spine. At last it occurred to him that he would make it of steel, and he took an oval stay bracing-wire for the purpose. It was about eight feet long, and he thought rigid enough.

When he had decided this and had unscrewed the stay, he found that the sun had set, and he went happily to rest, thinking that he would soon get his kite made and that it would catch the eye of any Mongolians who chanced to cross the plain.

Next morning he set to work at once on the kite, but when he had been at work an hour he changed his plan and decided to make a box kite. For this he needed four stays and four cross-members to hold them apart, and he thought that he had done well at the end of the day when he had got the skeleton of his kite complete, for he had had to cut a deep notch at the end of each of his cross-members, which would have been impossible if he had not made them by splitting a piece of spruce, instead of using steel.

He went to bed satisfied with himself, but exhausted, and got little rest that night. The next morning he began to cover his kite, which took him most of the day, because he had no needle and could not make one. Instead of a needle he sewed with an awl and a waxed thread, but to get the thread he had to unpick a sewn piece of doped aeroplane fabric, and could not often get it more than a foot long. At the end of the day the kite was made, and only then did he think of the string. But there is string in plenty on every aeroplane: kite string lacing the fabric cover on to the fuselage. He had only to set to work to unwind it from the eyelet hooks. Yet, when he had unwound it all, it seemed that it would not be enough, so he began the tedious job of unwrapping the string covering of the big oil-pipe, which protects the oil from being cooled too rapidly at high altitudes.

The next morning when he got up he took his kite up to the top of the bluff, but there was no wind. The sun was already scorching hot and there was not a cloud nor a bird visible in the sky. The stones shone and dazzled him. There was no life in the desert. In the weakness which had been growing on him during the last two days he was ready to despair, and put the kite away saying to himself angrily:

'I shall not live more than another few days and I have taken so much pains for nothing, except to prove how stupid I am. And the stupidest part about it is that even if I could fly the kite, it would not do me any good. I cannot live on water much longer. I am going to croak.'

The rest of the day he did not care to look at his kite and not being able to endure the heat of the sun, lay all day under the wing of the 'plane. The next day there was not a breath of wind stirring, and it seemed to him that his kite would never be flown at all unless someone found it and flew it after his death.

When he had drunk his breakfast allowance of water, it occurred to him that he would lose count of the days if he did not keep a diary. He therefore reckoned up the number of days that he had been in that place and wrote them down. After he had done this, it seemed clear to him that Shap and Mrs. Beanlands had not found any natives, or if they had, then any rescue party which had set out must have turned back. They would not find him after such a long interval, but it seemed possible that aeroplanes might yet come to search, particularly if the bodies of Mrs. Beanlands and Shap had not been found.

'I must eat soon or croak!' he said in a loud voice, and, taking his log-book, wrote down: '*Latest date for food to be any good is the day after to-morrow, Wednesday.*' After this point had been settled, he took his automatic pistol and the Very light pistol, so that he could signal in case an aeroplane should come over when he was at some distance from his beacon, and set out down the bed of the river to see if he could find any signs of game. When he had walked about half a mile the river-bed became full of big boulders, and he found walking difficult, and after slipping once and hurting his bad foot, he stopped to rest, and his thoughts which had for several days been exclusively occupied by the present and the future returned to the past, and he saw vividly the aerodrome and the club-house where he had eaten his last real meal.

'Think of it: that's still going on just the same. Tug, the instructor, tired and bored to death by bad pupils, is going round on circuits all the afternoon. Mrs. Parker goes solo. Cohen needs advanced instruction. Miss Pimple has to do spins next time there's too much wind for her to do landings. What a life! What a world! Poor old Tug. If there's one thing in the world he's certain of, it's that *The Tatler* is better reading than *The Sketch*—or *The Sketch* better than *The Tatler*. Just imagine, I've forgotten which it is! What a life! What a dull hole England is! Left-hand circuits round that aerodrome all day and a game of bridge in the club-house or a pub-crawl in the evening.

'The Groom and Horses is the spiciest place in this burg. Come along, Jimmy, we're going to investigate.'

My God, what a deadly life those fellows lead. If I do survive I hope to heaven mine will be a bit more like . . . like this.

He laughed at this strange conclusion to his thought and lifted his head, and as he did so a small hawk flew overhead, off the bluff. He fired at it at once, but his aim was not good; it is difficult in any case to shoot flying with an automatic pistol. But though he missed the hawk he was very greatly encouraged by having seen the bird, for he argued that he had now seen two birds of prey, and that there must be ground game on which they could live.

'Why are there no lizards?' he asked himself. 'That is extraordinary indeed. There should be lizards and snakes, and both can be eaten at a pinch.' From this time on his thoughts ran chiefly on hunting, and brought with them the inconvenience that he could not control the flow of his saliva and was always spitting and swallowing to be rid of it. After he had seen the hawk he came slowly back to the wrecked aeroplane, picking his way very carefully over the loose boulders for fear that he should twist his ankle again and be unable to go hunting on the morrow.

It had been a hot, absolutely windless day, but in the afternoon the wind began to blow gently from the south and it was hot in his mouth and on his skin. On the previous day such a wind would have rejoiced him, since he was thinking then only of flying his kite, but he no longer cared about it and did not bother to climb up to the bluff or to stir out of his cabin under the wing. When he did peer out the sky seemed to foreshadow a break in the weather for it had darkened, though without any cloud showing or the sunlight diminishing. For a few moments he wondered whether it might not be the prelude to an eclipse of the sun, but he remembered that eclipses do not last much more than an hour from first to last. By five o'clock in the afternoon (by what he thought the local time) the sky had grown a strange brown colour, and he feared that a great storm was about to break out.

'I should have unfastened the whole of the other wing of the aeroplane and have carried it bodily up on to the bluff. If there is a great downpour this *wady* may fill suddenly and wash me and the 'plane itself away while I am asleep. I should have little chance in such a wild rush of waters.'

While this fear was still bothering him, and he was resolving that if it were to rain really hard it would be more sensible to sleep in the open on the bluff, the sound of a few heavy drops on the 'plane over his head startled him by their force and weight.

'It is more like hail than rain; I must see that I have not left anything in the open which will be damaged. But danger or no, I'm damned if I sleep out in a hailstorm.' And he was surprised, because the air was still hot and scorching and the wind was from the south, all of which made hail seem unlikely.

Thinking these thoughts, he began to crawl out through the little doorway he had left in his cabin (after he had walled it), and while he was on his hands and knees in the entrance he was surprised to see a big brown grasshopper just in front of him.

'Hullo, what are you doing?' he asked the insect; and quickly, before it could jump, he caught it, and, without reflecting, broke off its head while it was still looking at him, and then, pulling off the legs and wings, popped it into his mouth. It was bitter and oily, but it seemed to him good because it was food and the first solid thing he had swallowed for more than a week. All this happened while he was still on his knees in the doorway of his cabin, but as soon as he was outside he saw that the ground was covered with other grasshoppers or locusts. They were perched on the tops of the big pebbles, sitting crosswise, or on the rounded sides of them, with their heads tipping up or down and in their folded-up state, with their round ends (their faces), they looked like large brown pocket-knives. It was queer to see so many living creatures suddenly in a place so barren. They did not jump about but sat still where they had fallen, composing themselves, and then crawling tentatively a step or two on to the top of a pebble.

The smooth upper surface of the 'plane was dotted over with their long bodies, and he understood suddenly that what he had thought were hailstones were really locusts. There were locusts in the air also, falling thinly with expanded wing-cases and feebly whirring glassy wings.

He caught another of them and mechanically killed it, peeled it of wings and legs and chewed it up.

'Food. They are food. I am saved,' he said, but they were not tolerable uncooked, and he began to catch and kill a number of the insects, killing them by breaking their heads off with his nail and throwing their bodies into the leather case of the thermos flask which Mrs. Beanlands had left behind. When he had caught and killed a couple of dozen of them, he stopped to build himself a fire with a few strips of spruce and shreds of doped aeroplane fabric. Over this he sprinkled a little petrol and lit it with his cigarette-lighter. It flared up violently, wasting itself while he sought feverishly for a steel wire on which he threaded the locusts and held them out to toast.

They scorched quickly; their wings burnt away and the lower joints of their legs; then their armour-plated bellies grew glossy and transparent with oil and they split like little sausages, and a smell more delicious than anything he had ever savoured came from them. It was a smell like fish, like freshwater fish, something like grilled trout. His mouth was running now with sweet saliva, his eye was wet with a big tear and his fingers shaking feverishly. He could not wait for them to cool before he began to eat them, and he burned himself the more since his mouth had grown unapt to hot things.

The locusts were delicious cooked, tasting like a mixture of shrimps and sausages and baked bananas. When he had toasted and eaten all that he had caught, he set to work to catch some more. He was in a frenzy and pursued them in the fury of his appetite, fearing that they might all take wing and depart suddenly. In his haste he no longer bothered to kill them cleanly, but crushed and maimed the insects by breaking off legs or head indiscriminately, and throwing the bodies rapidly on to the heap he was collecting, and pursuing them on hands and knees. At that rate it was not long before he had made himself a heap of dead and living broken bodies which would have filled a gallon measure, and with these he was content for the time, and only puzzled himself how to cook them quicker than by toasting them two or three at a time on a wire. He must roast them on a hot plate, and picking up his screwdriver and hammer he began to lever off an aluminium footplate from the top of the damaged wing, a plate which served to step on when the petrol tank was being filled. But before he had wrenched this off another idea came to him, and he unfastened a disc from one of the wheels and poured his locusts into that. Soon his fire was lighted anew and he was engaged in roasting a great mass of the insects, raking them over and over with a screwdriver as they became scorched too much on one side.

While he was eating them tears welled up continually in his eye; he was beside himself in an ecstasy of satisfaction and impatience and he gorged upon the food, and when they were all gone he was not content but had to set about catching another bagful and roasting another dish, and these also were eaten in the same way.

By that time it was too dark for him to see to collect any more of the insects, but for a while he delayed going to rest and sat watching the last embers of his fire burning away to ash. Sitting there he fell asleep.

Half an hour later he woke up with terrible pains in his stomach. He was sick continually, and in such agony that he could not stifle his moans. This lasted until nearly morning, when he was able to feel his way across to the runnel and get himself a drink of water and sponge the perspiration off his forehead and wash his hands.

In this way he was taught that he must be moderate after his fast, and although he was so weak that he could scarcely move, he was about directly he could see, in the first light before dawn, collecting the sleeping locusts in bagfuls, for he thought with terror that when the sun rose the swarm would take wing and fly away, leaving him with no more provision than he had before they came. The locusts did indeed rise up and fly on, but as other locusts began dropping soon after midday there was no great diminution in the supply. During early morning, and in the course of the day, he caught and killed nearly a bushel of the insects, working until he was almost fainting with exhaustion, but he did not eat any, since he was determined to control his appetite and diet himself until his stomach was normal.

While he was at work during the afternoon, slipping and sliding over the loose round stones, scaring the locusts to take wing at his approach, and batting them down with a piece of plywood, he rested for a moment and, looking up, saw a stream of about a dozen birds flying overhead. They travelled rapidly, and it seemed to him that they were pursuing a thin curtain of locusts, which, warping on the eastern wind, had passed over a little while before. The birds were soon out of sight behind the bluff, but Jimmy stood for some time, hoping to see them again, and watching the travelling locusts which so much resembled a travelling curtain of falling rain. During that evening and the succeeding days, he frequently saw birds of different kinds, which were following the locusts and feeding on them. Some of the birds were about the size of English starlings, but had rose-coloured breasts; the few which he saw on the ground, running about and eating locusts, seemed to be ordinary English starlings.

It gave him a great deal of pleasure whenever he saw these birds; they were evidence, he thought, that he was near the edge of the desert, but perhaps the real reason of his pleasure was because they were a familiar sort of bird, which is found near houses and in gardens and orchards, and he felt less lonely after he had seen them. The nearest he ever got to any of these birds was forty or fifty yards, and though a starling is a poor target for an automatic at that range, he would doubtless have shot at them if he had not been busy catching locusts at the time.

That evening he ate not more than a dozen roasted locusts, which tasted even more delicious than they had done the previous night, perhaps because he took a good deal more care in cooking them. After this meal he could not sleep for hunger for several hours.

Next morning he made himself a meal of forty locusts and felt no ill-effects. As the sun rose the insects took wing, and were almost all gone by ten o'clock, but other locusts began dropping all through the late afternoon. He collected another heap and saw that with what he had got he would be saved for many days to come. But he saw also that it was no good his catching a fortnight's supply of locusts if he could not cure them and keep them from going rotten. Had he possessed either salt or vinegar, or oil, it would have been easy, but lacking all condiments he could only think of one method, viz., of parching them by roasting them as slowly as possible on a hot plate over the embers and then packing them tightly in bags.

For this purpose he sacrificed the leather seat cushions, turning them inside out. At the end of the day's work he had one cushion stuffed tight with cured locusts, and a second about a third full. He had worked hard all day and was beginning to be alarmed because he had used so much of his fuel. To economise it, he determined only to make a fire when he was curing a large number of the insects at once.

The next morning he woke early and again collected locusts, but did not get more than half a gallon. While he was gathering them he noticed many among them thrusting their tails down between the stones, and standing with their hind legs raised anxiously off the earth in the air. This attitude struck Jimmy as funny. He thought that they were relieving themselves, and they reminded him of dogs when they are about the same business.

But as soon as the sun was well up the insects were off, rising in little clouds, circling round and joining in the larger cloud which swarmed from off the bluff and circled high above the river-bed. By mid-day there was not a living locust to be found any-where. During the afternoon and evening not a single insect fell in the river-bed, nor could he detect any swarms passing overhead. The locusts were gone, and Wreaks was able to wash himself all over in the runnel. He knew that he could support life for a month on what he had got, and his whole character was changed. He whistled as he splashed his naked body, and he laughed coarsely thinking of his return to London. For the first time since their departure he began to speculate disinterestedly about Mrs. Beanlands and Commander Shap.

'Of course, he was after her money. He hated fly-ing, but she was aching for a hero and for adventure. I guess she was brought up on Ethel Dell, and see what she came to. *The Way of an Eagle*. Not 'alf.'

Did Shap and Lily make love to each other in the desert? Wreaks felt inclined to doubt it. 'Dear Wil-mot would have been sweating with funk, if that desert is anything like it looks like. He wouldn't be feeling romantic, and, of course, poor Lily would be dog-tired, though she would be wanting love all the more. . . . It was rotten bad luck for her, and, God knows, I don't like to think of the end. . . . Of course they may be munching locusts just as I am.'

The rumblings of his gut and the calls of nature filled Wreaks with delight; they were all a proof of health and of the fact that he was going to survive. Of that he was convinced. He was a completely changed man. However, he made one discovery which upset him. As he was roasting the latest of his captures, the uncured fresh locusts, that evening he found many of them which were nearly empty. They were light; there was no substance in them. For a little while he feared that those he had cured might be the same, but he was soon reassured. The locusts he had cured were heavy; they were full of meat. He hit upon the explanation of this the next day.

While he was sitting on the shelving foot of the bluff, playing knucklebones, one of the stones chanced to fall and roll a few yards away from him, and he went after it on his hands and knees to pick it up.

Beside where the stone had come to rest was one of the crouching locusts with its head crushed but its abdomen thrust into the earth. His mood was idle as he picked it up, and then he saw that there was a string issuing from its tail, and, attached to this thread, swinging in the air, a little packet much the shape of a bundle of sausages. These were clearly the eggs which the mother locust must have been in the act of laying when he had chanced to crush her with his foot.

This packet was about the size of a haricot bean, and, as he examined it, he understood the reason why some of the locusts had been so light and empty, and he guessed that the eggs would be the best part, as the roe is of fish.

He therefore began stirring the stones about on the bank and soon found other egg-packets. These he roasted for his lunch but found they were too dry, so in the afternoon he collected about half a pint more, and these he boiled in the top of the thermos flask and found them very good and tender, and a delicious change after the parched and toasted insects. It was pleasant, also, to be eating a food which did not need picking over and shelling. Eating the roasted locusts always took him some time and left the stones littered over with the remains. It was like nothing so much as eating shrimps.

For three days he lived idly, rioting in food and enjoying his new carnality. Already he was planning to set out across the desert, carrying his bags of locusts with him and a supply of water in one of the tires of the aeroplane slung round his body like a bandolier. Then one morning, when he woke up, he noticed that there was a fresh breeze blowing. This was the long-sought opportunity to fly his kite and taking it up with a laugh, he climbed up to his beacon.

The wind was hot and southerly, and the kite lifted off the edge of the bluff and drew swiftly upwards in the up-current, and pride and joy in his kite filled him against his better judgement, for what good could the thing do him?

How it rushed upwards! How it gleamed silver against the blue! How it tugged at the string which was almost cutting into his finger! How fresh it was, how powerful, how it rode upon the air! As he watched the kite rising and falling, and growing smaller as the ball of string unrolled on the ground, he felt a lump rise in his throat. He sat down abruptly on the bluff's edge and, throwing a quick turn of the string about the calf of his leg to hold the kite, he put his hands over his face and wept out of his solitary eye. The pathos of his situation was too much; for a few moments he could not master his self-pity.

Then, without looking up at the kite, he paid out the rest of the string slowly and anchored the kite by fastening the end of it to the strut, which he thrust deeply into the ground.

'What-ho! She bumps!' he said aloud, giving the kite a defiant look. 'Someone may see that and call to inquire.'

Before six o'clock that evening the sky darkened suddenly to a coppery-brown colour, and the light seemed to throw primrose shadows on the sides of the white stones. There was the distant sound of rushing wind, of a shrill rustle which comes before a gale.

'I am in for a real storm this time,' Wreaks exclaimed, and started up the side of the cliff to haul down his kite. But before he had climbed a third of the way up a sudden flurry of locusts began to fall. He descended again to the aeroplane in surprise, and the weight of the strange tempest was upon him. Down, down, down, they rained, they drove, slowly as falling snow, thick as the thickest whirlwind of packed flakes, and the sound of their wings was loud and shrill and more lonely than the silence of falling snow.

His coat was covered with them in a moment; as they struck him on his face, they scratched it with knee and claw; he brushed them quickly off his mouth, his ear, his eyebrow; they crunched under his feet.

For a little while he laughed, delighted, exulting in their numbers. He thought he would collect enough locusts to last him six months and would tramp back to civilisation, munching them. But in five minutes he was exasperated by locusts, and dived into his cabin to be out of their way. The place was full of the insects sitting queerly about at different angles on his clothes, with their horse-like faces watching him, and their bent legs sticking sharply above the line of their backs like the folding button-hook in the pocket-knife.

He had brought a lot of them in with him on his clothes. For five minutes he busied himself in clearing the place of them, killing them with finger and thumb, and throwing them aside. But the number of them in the cabin did not decrease. In the queer yellow light, which came from the sun's light being filtered through the million wing-cases of their fellows, they looked curiously sinister and ugly.

'Ah! you automatic beasts! Why are there so many of you?'

Wreaks looked up out of his cabin and watched them pouring down with their expanded wing-cases, their whirring wings and long dangling legs. He could hear them, the shrill sound of the whirring wings, and the little flops of those nearest to him, dropping by pure chance anywhere, as they drifted blindly on to any object in their way without making any attempt to alight gracefully. And below the sound of their whirring wings he could distinguish the persistent rustle, as they folded their wings and drew themselves up into the correct sitting posture.

Suddenly Wreaks saw that the wreck of the aeroplane was checking them as they floated down and making a drift of them. They were a foot deep all along the foot of the bluff and they were eighteen inches deep round the wheels of the 'plane. There was a locust squashing down the back of his shirt, a locust in each ear; his hair was full of them. Quickly he combed them off with his fingers, and pulled on his flying-helmet and his goggles, and, thus protected, he plunged out among them. Those drifting in the air covered him, a few hopped off him or hopped on him, but most remained where they had fallen, drawing up their legs, turning their necks, staring. One scratched his nose, one he saw sitting sphinx-like on his sleeve until it suddenly bit a piece out of the material of his cuff.

He could no longer see the sun even as a radiance in a sky which was as brown as the thickest London fog: against its dimness the descending rain of living bodies was only feebly outlined; as it grew thicker it became darker, until in the brown light it was hard to see the insects when they had fallen on the reddish-brown carpet of their fellows. A sour, dirty smell sickened him; the shrill whirring of millions of wings deafened him.

Shouting oaths, Wreaks stood by the airscrew and slashed at them. But the sound of his own curses only maddened him, and roused in him a lust for massacre and destruction which he could not gratify. What was the use of striking down a hundred when the sky was stained bronze by billions of them? An insect alighted in his open mouth as he uttered a last curse, and he spat it out, suddenly sickened.

Yet he would kill and kill, and he stood striking angrily, exhausting himself with futile blows, until suddenly a better idea occurred to him. Since the crash he had pulled the tail of the machine down to the ground-level, and the propellor swung clear of the ground, and now he pulled himself swiftly to the cockpit and thrust in the plunger to dope the engine. Then he climbed out and, using all his strength, pulled the airscrew over five times to suck in petrol and get compression. Then he climbed back into the cockpit, switched on the impeller magneto, and got the engine to fire with the inertia starter. It fired unsteadily, and jets of black fumes were shot from the exhaust, then the sound changed to a gathering roar, and that blessed sound of power was lovely after the shrill rustle of desert locusts' wings! Man was speaking and challenging Nature.

He switched on the second magneto and opened the throttle. The broken, crazy skeleton of the 'plane rocked and shuddered and stuck against the boulders on which he had propped it up. The roar of the engine rose to a tornado of sound, in which the drumming of the exhaust and the scream of the propellor tips could be distinguished. The air was sucked back and hurled backwards in a furious gale, and at each of the turns hundreds of locusts fell mown down, killed and maimed, smashed into cream, or only slightly injured, and their bodies collected in a rapidly mounting heap.

'That's the way to kill 'em. Blast them, blast them, damn them. That's the way,' he shouted, unable to hear his own voice above the engine's roar. He had left it at full throttle.

Suddenly a stone gave way, the 'plane lurched forward sideways and fell drunkenly, the airscrew caught on a boulder and was shivered into a dozen fragments, and a flame ran in a flash from the engine to the wing like a flicker of lightning, which was followed by a light *poof* just audible above the roar. Without a word Wreaks, who had been watching and exulting in the massacre from the cockpit, jumped clear of the fuselage. Swift as a hare he threw himself into his cabin under the wing and dashed out with his flying-suit, which he hurled away. The flame leapt high above the central section of the wing; he could hear it crackle and roar up in flame over his stooped head as he dived into his cabin for the second time to retrieve his automatic and the pistol with Very lights, and a cushion full of parched locusts.

He pulled all these possessions away and stood, knee-deep in living locusts, which began to crawl up him as he stood, silently watching the destruction of all his hopes. The sun was setting; already the dusk had fallen and still the flames leapt higher and higher up, and their light was reflected in the horny eyes of millions of sun-worshippers.

As he watched the flames dancing along the fuselage and licking up from the fins of the 'plane, the locusts climbed on him unheeded until he was covered in them, clinging as thick all over him as swarming bees upon a branch.

At last he noticed them, shaking his head and waking from the contemplation of his own folly to the feeling of their teeth nipping his hair, his skin, his untrimmed savage beard, testing every part of him with a sharp nibble to find if it held the moisture for which the insects were dying.

Wildly he shook himself then, and combed the clustering ranks from head and shoulder, from back

and arm, and then, dancing in the light of the last flames of the burning 'plane, gesticulating like a lunatic, he gathered up the few things which he had saved and set out to climb the bluff. Its sides were practically free of insects, and he breathed for a moment with returning sanity. But when his fingers chanced to touch on one of the locusts clustering in the bundle of clothes he was carrying, he gave a convulsive shudder so violent that he nearly lost his balance. Then he swore furiously and stumbled on again, forcing himself to keep control and to fight back the madness of horror and the fury of remorse at his own folly.

He paused by the edge of the cliff and, groping carefully, felt his way to the piled slats and shreds of plywood and doped fabric of the beacon, which was all that he had left now in the world. Putting out his hand he touched the heap and grasped a locust between thumb and forefinger. He threw it aside with a wriggle of horror which shamed his efforts at control, and then pulled out his petrol cigarette-lighter and snapped it to look. The wick caught and the feeble flame flickered and threw a light which was reflected in a thousand points: every splinter of wood and carelessly piled spar, and squarer section of three-ply, bore its clustered living freight, holding on crosswise, head up or down, hanging at every angle like the crystals of rime upon a hoar-frosted bush in England.

For a moment he was so disgusted that he was tempted to burn up these also with the flame held so near to them, but he laughed at his own folly and, drawing back, clicked down the lid extinguishing the flame.

Afterwards it was lighted again, and for a little while, like a will-o'-the-wisp, the flame searched up and down along the edge of the bluff, where scarcely any insects were roosting for the night, the majority having fallen down to join the ghastly drift below, or floated on a few farther yards on to the level of the plain.

The few locusts he found, Wreaks swept away with his swung leather suit, which he afterwards put on before he lay down on the bare earth, gazing at the last glowing embers of the 'plane beneath him.

In the morning when he woke his first impression was of this dizzy height, for he had moved nearer to the brink of the cliff while he was sleeping and he was almost overhanging it when he opened his eyes.

The sun was up, and the locusts were already moving, he had been awakened indeed by one of them which had dropped with a thud and scratch upon his cheek. He rolled back from the cliff and turned his head, and from the piled sticks of his beacon he saw a few insects rise on whirring transparent wings and circle, and heard also the stridulating music, their morning prayer, the first anthem of their Lord the Sun-god.

The sound came very faintly to his ears, he sat up and pulled off his leather helmet, and at once the anthem pealed louder, louder, and with a shout he sprang to his feet and, standing rigidly, he listened.

The voice which had caught his ear had dwindled, but he stood motionless, refusing to believe that he might have been mistaken, or that he was mad, and searching the distant blue spaces of the sky.

As he gazed, he saw a gathering whirlwind of rising locusts that rose up in a great vortex, staining the blueness of the sky, and as he listened the drone of a deeper stridulation struck on his ears.

The flame of the petrol-lighter caught at the beacon and a tongue of fire licked the live locusts as it soared upwards—all unnecessary. The green Very light shot into an arc of the sky and the roar of the suddenly visible aeroplane came in answer.

Round the bluff it swooped, banking and circling and diving in a swift silence, and a waved arm answered his waved salute.

'A Moth. A Moth. A bloody little Moth!' he whispered.

The engine roared out once more and the machine tore away across the broken rocks of the plain. A few minutes later it was back and circled over him again, and once more flew straight off towards the east. 'He's got a place to land on over there; he wants me to follow.'

Wreaks made a hasty preparation and set off a few minutes later after it, taking with him only his brandy flask full of water, his two pistols and a pocketful of parched locusts.

While he was still within a few hundred yards of where he had started, the machine returned once more.

'Stout fellow. He doesn't mean to lose sight of me.'

On this occasion the machine came down in a glide to within a few feet of Wreaks, who was able to nod and yell his comprehension to the pilot, before he pushed open his throttle and roared away up the line of the river to the mountains in the east.

Jimmy had a twelve-mile walk before he reached the cliffs and found a way up them without difficulty. While he was climbing, the 'plane came again to look for him, but after coming close to him, it turned back and disappeared over the top of the cliff.

He climbed on, and when he reached the top he

found himself on a level sandy plateau stretching to the mountains. Not two hundred yards from where he stood was the Moth aeroplane with the airscrew ticking over quietly and a helmeted goggled figure climbing out. While Jimmy had been making his way over the broken country, jumping from rock to rock and running where he found a stretch of level sand, he had been happy and light-hearted, not thinking of the future in his excitement, and only laughing between his gasps for breath and repeating to himself in his excitement that he was saved.

But the sight of the slender little Moth, with its ticking airscrew, overcame him. It was too much like home. He tried to run towards it and did not know it when he stumbled and fell with weariness, but with his eye still fixed on the machine, picked himself up and tottered crazily on. His eye was full of tears; he blubbered weakly: 'My God, my God! how beautiful!'

But the 'plane was real. The engine went on ticking over as he approached, and the pilot was walking towards him. The pilot, however, was the surprise which pulled Jimmy together and saved him from an emotional breakdown. He was a Chinaman, rather a brown-skinned Chinaman, with black squint eyes, and he was laughing, making an odd, hissing noise.

'What! You are English? I thought you would be a Russian. Well, that machine is English. I learned to fly in England. I was at Cambridge.' They shook hands, and it was a moment or two before Jimmy could bring himself to let go. Once he had touched another human being he wanted to keep hold. Then he suddenly became normal, and they talked. It turned out that Jimmy had been very lucky.

Mr. Huan Lang had been flying for one of the generals of the Northern Army. 'Then peace came —an armistice—and since the General is a very enlightened man who follows science, he sent me to watch and report on the locust swarms. They were doing an immense damage to some not-far-distant cotton estates. I followed them. I followed them three hundred miles, and last night, just as I was going to say good-bye to them, I saw your 'plane burning.

So this morning I came back to see if there was anyone left alive.'

But this story ends here, months before Jimmy Wreaks will stoop to unlatch the low little front-garden gate. He will push the bell of the lower maisonette, and his wife will open it. There will be a hopeless sort of smile on her pale, troubled face; and he will give her his ugly unfortunate smile and will say apologetically:

'I've been an awful long time getting back on this trip, Daphne!'

'Yes, I know, I know. That poor woman. . . . Well, aren't you coming in, Jimmy?'

'No, I just stopped in to see you for a minute and to leave my bag. . . . Now I'll go on to the 'drome. I'll be back in a couple of hours.'

'I'll slip out and get a haddock for your supper.'

'Cheerioh.'

'Cheerioh, Jimmy.'

That will not come to pass for many months, but Jimmy has stepped up on to the lower wing and has climbed into the front cockpit and has strapped himself in and waved his arm to the pilot behind.

The throttle roared wide open; the little Moth raced across the sand, and carelessly, dangerously, swung off the earth and after a moment or two put up her nose to climb steeply into the sky.

Steeply, oh so steeply she climbed, shooting up behind her roaring Gipsy engine into a blue, empty Chinese sky, framed by the Gobi desert on the north and the high Nan-shan ranges on the south. There was the roar of the Gipsy engine and the Moth climbing and the wind tearing at Jimmy's unprotected head, for he had forgotten to bring his helmet, and the wind was wringing tears out of his ungoggled eye.

'Christ, this Johnny is a bad pilot. He's scaring me stiff. I wish I were back with the grasshoppers! My nerves can't stand this. I must give him a few lessons.'

Oh joy, oh blessed world! They were in the sky, riding on the air, and all the groping dirtiness of earth forgotten.

Where the locusts had sojourned the desert was full of living seed: under the pebbles, in every crack in the shaly friable earth, were pushed the swollen egg-pods which broke asunder after they began to stir with life in the sun's heat and gave out the little creeping maggots.

Millions upon millions of individual living beings were scattered thus to writhe feebly and die in the vast sterility of the deserts. But where the parent swarm had favoured them by chancing on better lands, they flourished on the roots of grasses and sucked the sap of plants. Growing thus they appeared in the light of the sun, to crawl and grow and hop and devastate the earth.

Then this progeny of the swarm, those which had survived, gathered up in their clans and colonies and hopping faster and ever faster in the sun's rays, they jostled each other, and from their jostling in the heat of the day was begotten further hopping until band joined band, and legion legion, and, as the army multiplied, its movements became ordered by the pressure of one rank upon the next, and while the sun was hot they marched in serried masses at random. Down in the lush valleys the ignorant cattle crunched them complacently as they gnawed away the last blades of herbage from under their lips and passed on, leaving them to bellow and perish, and, going farther, they flowed round the weary ruined men who fought them with trenches and barricades, with flame and poisoned bait.

When they fell in waterless desert places they died; where they passed they left desert; they sprouted wings and flew. Their seed sprang again in wingless armies from the earth. They had no reason and little that might be called instinct. All their movements are due to the heat of the sun. They are thermotropic.

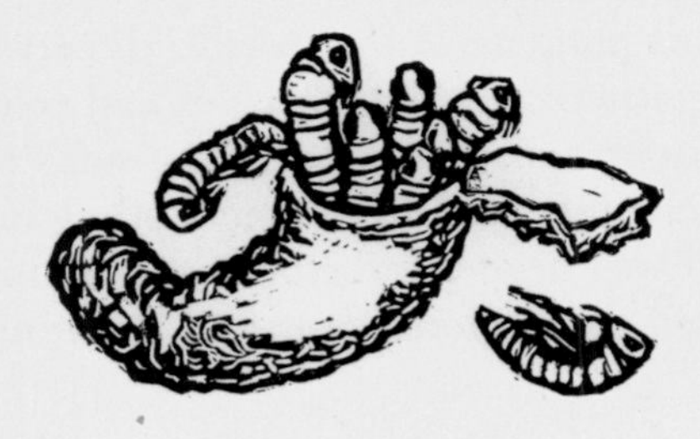